THE LIFE OF THE IMAGINATION

Hans thought about Heilner for the rest of the afternoon. Heilner had thoughts and words of his own, he lived a richer and freer life, suffered strange ailments and seemed to despise everything around him. He understood the beauty of the ancient columns and walls. And he practiced the mysterious and unusual art of mirroring his soul in verse and of constructing a semblance of life for himself out of his imagination. He was quick and untamable and had more fun in a day than Hans in an entire year. He was melancholy and seemed to relish his own sadness like an unusual condition, alien and delicious.

BENEATH THE WHEEL
BY HERMANN HESSE

BENEATH
THE WHEEL

HERMANN HESSE

Translated by Michael Roloff

BANTAM BOOKS
TORONTO · NEW YORK · LONDON · SYDNEY

*This low-priced Bantam Book
has been completely reset in a type face
designed for easy reading, and was printed
from new plates. It contains the complete
text of the original hard-cover edition.*
NOT ONE WORD HAS BEEN OMITTED.

BENEATH THE WHEEL

*A Bantam Book / published by arrangement with
Farrar, Straus and Giroux, Inc.*

PRINTING HISTORY

*Translated from the German, Unterm Rad, originally published
in 1906 From Gesammelte Schriften, Copyright 1953 by
Hermann Hesse, Montagnola*
Farrar edition published June 1968
2nd printing ...... October 1968

Bantam edition / October 1970

2nd printing ... October 1971	*6th printing .. November 1975*
3rd printing ... January 1972	*7th printing . September 1976*
4th printing ... October 1972	*8th printing ... January 1979*
5th printing ...... May 1973	*9th printing . September 1980*
	10th printing .... November 1981

ISBN 0-553-20858-6

Published simultaneously in the United States and Canada

*Bantam Books are published by Bantam Books, Inc. Its trade-
mark, consisting of the words "Bantam Books" and the por-
trayal of a rooster, is Registered in U.S. Patent and Trademark
Office and in other countries. Marca Registrada. Bantam
Books, Inc., 666 Fifth Avenue, New York, New York 10103.*

PRINTED IN THE UNITED STATES OF AMERICA

19 18 17 16 15 14 13 12 11 10

BENEATH THE WHEEL

Chapter One

HERR JOSEPH GIEBENRATH, jobber and middleman, possessed no laudable or peculiar traits distinguishing him from his fellow townsmen. Like the majority, he was endowed with a sturdy and healthy body, a knack for business and an unabashed, heartfelt veneration of money; not to mention a small house and garden, a family plot in the cemetery, a more or less enlightened if threadbare attachment to the church, an appropriate respect for God and the authorities, and blind submission to the inflexible laws of bourgeois respectability. Though no teetotaler, he never drank to excess; though engaged in more than one questionable deal, he never transgressed the limits of what was legally permitted. He despised those poorer than himself as have-nots and those wealthier as show-offs. He belonged to the Chamber of Commerce and every Friday went bowling at the Eagle. He smoked only cheap cigars, reserving a better brand for after-dinner and Sundays.

In every respect, his inner life was that of a Philistine. The "sensitive" side of his personality had long since corroded and now consisted of little more than a traditional rough-and-ready "family sense," pride in his only son, and an occasional charitable impulse toward the poor. His intellectual gifts were limited to an inborn canniness and dexterity with figures. His reading was confined to the newspapers, and his need for amusement was assuaged by the amateur theatricals the Chamber of Commerce put on each year and an occasional visit to the circus. He could have exchanged his name and address with any of his neighbors, and nothing would have been different. In common with every other paterfamilias in town, and deeply ingrained in his soul, he also had this: deepseated distrust of any power or person superior to himself, and animosity toward anyone who was either extraordinary or more gifted, sensitive or intelligent than he.

Enough of him. It would require a profound satirist to represent the shallowness and unconscious tragedy of this man's life. But he had a son, and there's more to be said about him.

Hans Giebenrath was, beyond doubt, a gifted child. One gathered as much simply by noting the subtle and unusual impression he made on his fellow students. Their Black Forest village was not in the habit of producing prodigies. So far it had not brought forth anyone whose vision and effect had transcended its narrow confines. Only God knows where this boy got his serious and intelligent look and his elegant movements. Had he inherited them

from his mother? She had been dead for years
and no one remembered anything special about
her, except that she had always been sickly and unhappy. As for coming from the father, that was
out of the question. For once it seemed that a spark
from above had struck this old hamlet which, in
the eight or nine centuries of its existence, had
produced many a stalwart citizen but never a
great talent or genius.

A trained observer, taking note of the sickly
mother and the considerable age of the family,
might have speculated about hypertrophy of the
intelligence as a symptom of incipient degeneration. But the little town was fortunate in not having anyone so trained in its midst; only the younger
and more clever civil servants and teachers had
heard uncertain rumors or read magazine articles
about the existence of "modern" man. It was possible to live in this town and give the appearance
of being educated without knowing the speeches
in *Zarathustra*. The town's entire mode of existence had an incurably old-fashioned character;
there were many well-founded and frequently
happy marriages. The long-established and well-to-
do citizens, many of whom had risen from the rank
of artisan to manufacturer within the last twenty
years, doffed their hats to the officials and sought
their company, but behind their backs spoke of
them as pen-pushers and poor bureaucrats. Yet
they had no higher ambition for their sons than a
course of study that would enable them to become

civil servants. Unfortunately, this was almost always a pipe dream, because their offspring often had great difficulty getting through grammar school and frequently had to repeat the same form.

There was unanimous agreement about Hans Giebenrath's talents, however. Teachers, principal, neighbors, pastor, fellow students and everyone else readily admitted that he was an exceptionally bright boy—something special. Thus his future was mapped out, for in all of Swabia there existed but one narrow path for talented boys—that is, unless their parents were wealthy. After passing the state examination, he could enter the theological academy at Maulbronn, then the seminary at Tübingen, and then go on to either the minister's pulpit or the scholar's lectern. Year after year three to four dozen boys took the first steps on this safe and tranquil path—thin, overworked, recently confirmed boys who followed the course of studies in the humanities at the expense of the state, eight or nine years later embarking on the second and longer period of their life when they were supposed to repay the state for its munificence.

The state examination was to be held in a manner of weeks. This annual hecatomb, during which the state took the pick of the intellectual flower of the country, caused numerous families in towns and villages to direct their sighs and prayers at the capital.

Hans Giebenrath was the only candidate our little town had decided to enter in the arduous

competition. It was a great but by no means unde-
served honor. Every day, when Hans completed
his classwork at four in the afternoon, he had an
extra Greek lesson with the principal; at six, the
pastor was so kind as to coach him in Latin and
religion. Twice a week, after supper, he received
an extra math lesson from the mathematics teacher.
In Greek, next to irregular verbs, special emphasis was placed on the syntactical connections as expressed by the particles. In Latin the onus rested
on a clear and pithy style and, above all, on master-
ing the many refinements of prosody. In mathematics the main emphasis was on especially complicated solutions. Arriving at these solutions, the
teacher insisted, was not as worthless for future
courses of study as might appear, for they sur-
passed many of his main subjects in providing
him with the basis for sober, cogent and successful
reasoning.

In order that Hans' mind not be overburdened
and his spiritual needs not suffer from these intellectual exertions, he was allowed to attend confirmation class every morning, one hour before
school. The catechism and the stimulating lessons
by rote introduced into the young soul a refreshing
whiff of religious life. Unfortunately, Hans les-
sened the potential benefit of these revivifying
hours by concealing in his catechism surreptitious
lists of Greek and Latin vocabulary and exercises,
and devoting the entire hour to these worldly
sciences. His conscience was not so blunted that

he did not feel uneasiness and fear, for when the deacon stepped up to him, or even called on him, he invariably flinched; and when he had to give an answer, he would break into a sweat and his heart would palpitate. Yet his answers were perfectly correct, as was his pronunciation, something which counted heavily with the deacon.

The assignments that accumulated from lesson to lesson during the course of the day he was able to complete later in the evening, at home, in the kindly glow of his lamp. These calm labors, under the aegis of these peaceful surroundings—a factor to which the classroom teacher assigned a particularly profound and beneficial effect—usually were not completed before ten o'clock on Tuesdays and Saturdays, on other days not before eleven or twelve. Though his father grumbled a little about the immoderate consumption of kerosene, he nonetheless regarded all this studying with a deep sense of personal satisfaction. During leisure hours on Sundays, which, after all, make up a seventh part of our lives, Hans had been urged to do outside reading and to review the rules of grammar.

"Everything with moderation, of course. Going for an occasional walk is necessary and does wonders," the teacher said. "If the weather is fine, you can even take a book along and read in the open. You'll see how easy and pleasant it is to learn that way. Above all, keep your chin up."

So Hans kept his chin as high as he could, and from that time on used his walks for studying. He could be seen walking quietly and timorously, with a nightworn face and tired eyes.

"What do you think of Giebenrath's chances? He'll make it, won't he?" the classroom teacher once asked the principal.

"He will, he most certainly will," exclaimed the principal joyously. "He's one of the extra-bright ones. Just look at him. He's the veritable incarnation of intellect."

During the last week, this intellectualization of the boy had become noticeable. Deep-set, uneasy eyes glowed dimly in his handsome and delicate face; fine wrinkles, signs of troubled thinking, twitched on his forehead, and his thin, emaciated arms and hands hung at his side with the weary gracefulness reminiscent of a figure by Botticelli.

The time was close at hand. Tomorrow morning he was to go to Stuttgart with his father and show the state whether he deserved to enter the narrow gate of the academy. He had just paid the principal a farewell visit.

"This evening," the feared administrator informed him with unusual mildness, "you must not so much as *think* of a book. Promise me. You have to be as fresh as a daisy when you arrive in Stuttgart. Take an hour's walk and then go right to bed. Young people have to have their sleep."

Hans was astonished to be the object of so much solicitude instead of the usual sally of admonitions, and he gave a sigh of relief as he left the school building. The big linden trees on the hill next to the church glowed wanly in the heat of the late afternoon sun. The fountains in the market square splashed and glistened. The blue-black fir and spruce-covered mountains rose up sharply behind the jagged line of roofs. The boy felt as if he had not seen any of this for a long time, and all of it struck him as unusually beautiful. True, he had a headache, but he did not have to study any more today.

He ambled across the square, past the ancient city hall through the lane that led to the market, past the cutler's shop, to the old bridge. He whiled away the time walking back and forth and finally sat down on the broad balustrade. For months on end he had passed this spot four times a day without as much as glancing at the small gothic chapel by the bridge, the river, the sluice gate, the dam or the mill, not even at the bathing meadow or the shore lined with willow trees where one tannery adjoined the other, where the river was as deep and green and tranquil as a lake and where the thin willow branches arched into the water.

He remembered how many hours, how many days and half days he had spent here, how often he had gone swimming or dived, rowed and fished here. Yes, fishing! He had almost forgotten what it was like to go fishing, and one year he had cried so bitterly when he'd been forbidden to, on account of the examination. Going fishing! That had been the best part of his school years. Standing in the shade cast by a willow at the edge of the tranquil spot near where the water cascaded over the dam; the play of light on the river, the fishing rod gently swaying; the rush of excitement when he had a bite and drew in his catch; the peculiar satisfaction when he held a cool fleshy fish wriggling in his hand.

Hadn't he caught many a juicy carp and whiting and barbel and delicate tench and many pretty shiners? He gazed for a long while across the water. The sight of this green corner of the river made him thoughtful and sad, and he sensed that the free and wild pleasures of boyhood were receding into the past. He pulled a hunk of bread from his pocket, divided it, rolled pellets of various sizes and tossed them into the water; they sank and the fish snapped at them. First the minnows and grayling came and devoured the smaller pieces, pushing the larger ones in front of them in zigzags. Then a somewhat larger whiting swam up cautiously, his dark back hardly distinguishable from the bottom, sailed around the pellet thoughtfully, suddenly let it disappear in his round mouth. A warm dampness rose from the lazily flowing river. A few light-colored clouds were dimly reflected in the green surface. The circular saw could be heard whining at the mill and the sound of water rushing over both dams flowed together into a deep sonorous roar. Hans' thoughts went back to the recent Sunday on which he had been confirmed and during which he had caught himself going over the conjugation of a Greek verb amidst the solemn festive occasion. He noticed that at other times recently his thoughts had become jumbled; even in school he invariably thought of the work just completed or just ahead, but never what he had to do that very moment. Well, that was just perfect for his exam!

Distracted he rose, undecided where to go next. He was startled when he felt a strong hand grasp his shoulder and a deep, friendly voice say: "Hello, Hans, you'll walk a way with me, won't you?"

That was Flaig, the shoemaker, at whose house he used to spend a few hours each evening, though he had neglected him for some time now. Hans joined him presently, however, without paying very close heed to what the devout Pietist was saying.

Flaig spoke of the examination, wished Hans good luck, and offered encouragement, but the real point of his speech was to communicate his firm belief that the examination was only an external and accidental event, which it would be no disgrace to fail. This could happen to the best of us, he said, and if it should happen to Hans he ought to keep in mind that God has a master plan for each and every soul and leads it along a path of His choosing,

Hans felt a bit queer whenever he was with Flaig. He respected him and his self-assured and admirable way of life, but everyone made so much fun of the Pietists that Hans had even joined in the laughter, though frequently against his own better judgment. Besides, he felt ashamed of his cowardice: he had been avoiding the shoemaker for some time, because he asked such pointed questions. Since Hans had become the teachers' pet and grown a bit conceited as a result, Master Flaig had looked at him oddly, as if to humiliate him. Thus the well-intentioned guide had gradually lost his sway over the boy's soul. For Hans was in the full bloom of boyish stubbornness and his antennae were most sensitively attuned to any unloving interference with his image of himself. Now he walked by Flaig's side and listened to him, oblivious of how kindly and anxiously he was being regarded.

In Crown Alley they encountered the pastor. The shoemaker gave him a curt greeting and was suddenly in a hurry. The pastor was one of the "modern" ones. He had the reputation of not even believing in the Resurrection. This man now took Hans by the hand.

"How are things," he asked. "You must be glad now that everything is almost over and done with."

"Oh yes, I'm pleased about that."

"Well, just take care of yourself. You know that we have high hopes for you. Especially in Latin I expect you to do well."

"But what if I fail?" Hans suggested shyly.

"Fail?" The good man stopped short. "Failing is absolutely out of the question. Completely impossible. What an idea!"

"I just mean it's a possibility. After all . . ."

"It isn't, Hans. It just isn't. Don't even think of it. And now give my regards to your father and take heart."

Hans watched him walk off. Then he turned around to see where the shoemaker had gone. What was it he had said? Latin wasn't all that important, provided your heart was in the right place and you trusted in God. A lot of help *he* was. And now the pastor, too, of all people! He couldn't possibly look him in the face again, if he failed.

Feeling depressed, he arrived home and went into their small garden. Here stood a rotting summer-house in which he had once built a rabbit hutch and raised rabbits for three years. Last fall they had been taken from him, on account of the examination. There had been no time left for distractions.

Nor had he been in the garden itself for some time. The empty rabbit cage looked dilapidated, the small wooden water wheel lay bent and broken by the conduit. He thought back to the time when he had built these things and had had fun with them. Even that lay two years back—an eternity. He picked up the small wheel, tried to bend it back into shape, but it broke completely and he flung it over the wall. Away with the stuff —it was all long over and done with. Then he suddenly remembered August, his friend from school, who had helped him build the wheel and cage. Whole afternoons they had played here, hunted with his slingshot, lain in ambush for cats, built tents and eaten raw turnips for supper. Then all the studying had left him no time. August had dropped out of school a year ago and become apprenticed to a mechanic; since then, he had come over to see Hans only twice. Of course, he too had less free time than before.

Cloud shadows hastened across the valley. The sun stood near the mountain edge. For just a second the boy felt like flinging himself to the ground and weeping. Instead he fetched the hatchet from the shed, swung it wildly with his thin arms, and smashed the rabbit hutch. The boards splintered, nails bent with a crunch, and a bit of mildewed rabbit feed from last year fell on the ground. He lashed out at it all as though this would crush his longing for the rabbits and for August and for all the old childish games.

"Now, now. What's going on there?" his father called from an open window.

"Making firewood!"

He gave no further reply but tossed the hatchet aside, ran through the yard to the street and then upstream along the river. Outside town, near the brewery, two rafts lay moored. He used to untie them and drift downstream for hours on warm Sunday afternoons, excited and lulled by the sound of water splashing between the loosely tied logs. He leaped across to the rafts, lay down on a heap of willows and tried to imagine the raft untied, rushing forward, slowing down in calmer waters along the meadows, coasting along fields, villages and cool forest edges, underneath bridges and through open locks, bearing him along and everything the way it used to be when he fetched rabbit feed along the Kapferberg, fished along the shore by the tanneries, without headaches and worries.

Tired and moody, he returned home for supper. Because of the imminent trip to Stuttgart, his father was wrought up and asked him at least a dozen times whether his books were packed, and his black suit laid out, and if he didn't want to read a grammar on the trip, and if he felt well. Hans gave terse, biting replies, ate little and soon bade his father good night.

"Good night now, Hans. Make sure you sleep well. I'll get you up at six. You haven't forgotten to pack your word book, have you?"

"No, I haven't forgotten to pack my dictionary. Good night, Father."

In the dark, he sat for a long time in his room. That was the only solace the whole examination business had brought him—a small room of his own. Here he was his own master, undisturbed. Here—obstinately, ambitiously—he had battled weariness, sleep and headaches, brooding many hours over Caesar, Xenophon, grammars, dictionaries and mathematics. But he had also experi-

enced those few hours more valuable than all lost
boyhood joys, those few rare, dreamlike hours
filled with the pride, intoxication and certainty of
victory; hours during which he had dreamed himself beyond school and examinations into the elect
circle of higher beings. He had been seized by a
bold and marvelous premonition that he was really
something special, superior to his fat-cheeked, good-
natured companions on whom he would one day
look down from distant heights. At this very moment, he breathed a sigh of relief, as though simply being in this room meant breathing a freer
and cooler air, and he sat down on his bed and
passed a few twilight hours with dreams, wishes
and anticipation. Slowly his eyelids slipped over
his big overworked eyes, opened once more, blinked
and fell shut again. The boy's pale head dropped
between his thin shoulders and his thin arms
stretched out, exhausted. He had fallen asleep
with his clothes on. The gentle, motherly hand
of sleep soothed the tempest in his heart and
smoothed the light wrinkles on his brow.

It was unheard of. The principal had taken the
trouble of coming to the station at such an early
hour. Herr Giebenrath in his black dress suit
could hardly stand still with excitement, happiness
and pride; he tiptoed nervously around the principal and Hans, accepted the stationmaster's and
railroad men's best wishes for the trip and his son's
examination, and kept switching a small suitcase

from right hand to left. His umbrella was held under his right arm, but he clamped it between his knees when switching the suitcase and it dropped a few times; whenever this happened, he set his suitcase down so he could pick up the umbrella. You would have thought he was an emigrant about to leave for America rather than the holder of round-trip tickets to Stuttgart for him and his son. Hans looked relaxed, though his throat was tight with apprehension.

The train pulled into the station, the two passengers mounted, the principal waved his hand to them, Hans' father lighted a cigar, and the little town and river gradually disappeared. The trip was sheer agony for both of them.

When they arrived at Stuttgart, his father suddenly came alive and seemed cheerful, affable and very much the man of the world. He was inspired by the excitement the man from a small town feels when he comes to the capital for a few days. Hans, however, became more afraid and quiet. He felt deeply intimidated by the sight of the city, the unfamiliar faces, the high, pompously ornate buildings, the long, tiring streets. The horse trams and the street noises frightened him. They were staying with an aunt, and the unfamiliarity of the rooms, her friendliness and loquacity, the endless sitting around and the never-ending remarks of encouragement directed at him by his father crushed the boy completely. Feeling lost and out of place, he sat in the room. When he looked at the un-

16

familiar surroundings, the aunt in her fashionable getup, the large-patterned wallpaper, the clock on the mantelpiece, the pictures on the walls, or when he gazed through the window onto the noisy bustling street, he felt completely betrayed. It seemed to him as though he had left home ages ago, and had forgotten everything he had learned with so much effort.

He had wanted to take a last look at his Greek particles in the afternoon, but his aunt suggested going for a walk. For a brief moment Hans envisioned something like green meadows and a forest in the wind and he cheerfully said yes. However, in no time at all he realized what a very different pleasure it is to take a walk in the city.

He and his aunt went walking without his father, who had gone to visit some acquaintances in town. Hans' misery began on the way downstairs. On the first floor they encountered a fat, overdressed lady to whom his aunt curtsied and who immediately broke into a stream of chatter. This pause lasted more than fifteen minutes. Hans stood to the side, pinned to the banister, was sniffed and growled at by the lady's lap dog, and vaguely comprehended that they also discussed him—the fat lady inspected him repeatedly through her lorgnette. They had hardly stepped into the street when his aunt entered a store and considerable time passed before she reemerged. Meanwhile Hans stood timidly by the curb, was jostled by passers-by and called names by the street boys.

Upon returning, his aunt handed him a chocolate bar and he thanked her politely even though he couldn't stand chocolate. At the next corner they mounted a horse tram and now they chugged in the overcrowded car through streets and more streets until they finally reached a broad avenue. A fountain was splashing, formal flower-beds were blossoming, goldfish swam in a small pond, an artificial one. You walked up and down, back and forth, and in a circle among swarms of other walkers. You saw masses of faces, elegant dresses, less elegant ones, bicycles, wheelchairs and perambulators, heard a babble of voices and inhaled warm dusty air. Finally you sat down on a bench next to other people. The aunt had been chattering away; now she sighed, smiled kindly at the boy and asked him to eat his chocolate. He didn't want to.

"My God, it doesn't embarrass you, does it? Go ahead, eat it."

Thereupon he pulled the little chocolate bar out of his pocket, tugged at the silver foil for a while and finally bit off a very small piece. He simply didn't care for chocolate but he dared not tell his aunt. While he was trying to swallow the piece, his aunt recognized someone in the crowd and rushed off.

"Just stay here. I'll be back in a jiffy...."

Hans used the opportunity to fling the chocolate on the lawn. Then he dangled his legs back and forth, stared at the crowd and felt unlucky. Finally he could think of nothing better to do than recite his irregular verbs but was horrified to discover that he had forgotten practically all of them. He had clean forgotten them! And tomorrow was the examination!

His aunt returned, having picked up the news that 118 boys would take the state examination this year and that only 36 could pass. At this point the boy's heart hit absolute rock bottom and he refused to say another word all the way back. At home his headache returned. He refused to eat anything and behaved so strangely that his father gave him a sharp talking to and even his aunt found him impossible. That night he slept deeply but badly, haunted by horrid nightmares: he saw himself sitting in a room with the other 117 candidates; the examiner, who sometimes resembled his pastor at home and then his aunt, kept piling heaps of chocolate in front of him which he was ordered to eat; as he ate, bathed in tears, he saw one candidate after the other get up and leave; they had all eaten their chocolate mountains while his kept growing before his eyes as if it wanted to smother him.

Next morning, while Hans sipped his coffee without letting the clock out of sight, he was the object of many people's thoughts in his home town. Shoemaker Flaig was the first to think of him. Before breakfast he said his prayers. The entire family, including the journeymen and the two apprentices, stood in a circle around the table, and to the usual morning prayer Flaig added the words: "Oh Lord, protect Hans Giebenrath, who is taking the state examination today. Bless and strengthen him so that he will become a righteous and sturdy proclaimer of your name."

Although the pastor did not offer a prayer in his behalf he said to his wife at breakfast: "Little Giebenrath is just about to start his exam. He's going to become someone very important one day, and it won't have hurt that I helped him with his Latin."

His classroom teacher before beginning the day's first lesson said to the other pupils: "So, the examination in Stuttgart is about to begin and we want to wish Giebenrath the best of luck. Not that he needs it. He's as smart as ten of you lazybones put together." And most of the pupils too turned their thoughts to the absent Hans, especially those who had placed bets on his failing or passing.

And because heartfelt prayers and deep sympathy easily take effect even over great distances, Hans sensed that they were thinking of him at home. He entered the examination room with trembling heart, accompanied by his father, anxiously followed the instructor's directions, and looking around the huge room full of boys, felt like a criminal in a torture chamber. But once the examining professor had entered and bid them be quiet, and dictated the text for the Latin test, Hans was relieved to find that it was ridiculously easy. Quickly, almost cheerfully, he wrote his first draft. Then he copied it neatly and carefully, and was one of the first to hand in his work. Though he managed to get lost on his way back to his aunt's house, and wandered about the hot streets for two hours, this did not upset his newly regained composure; he was glad to escape his aunt's and father's clutches for a while and felt like an adventurer as he ambled through the unfamiliar noisy streets of the capital. When he had asked his way back through the labyrinth and returned home, he was showered with questions.

"How did it go? What was it like? Did you know your stuff?"

"Couldn't have been easier," he said proudly. "I could have translated that in the fifth grade."

And he ate with considerable appetite.

He had no examination that afternoon. His father dragged him from one acquaintance or relative to the other; at one of their houses they met a shy boy who was dressed in black, an examination candidate from Göppingen. The boys were left to their own devices and eyed each other shyly and inquisitively.

"What did you think of the Latin?" asked Hans. "Easy, wasn't it?"

"But that's just it. You slip up when it's easy and don't pay attention and there are bound to have been some hidden traps."

"Do you think so?"

"But of course! The professors aren't as stupid as all that."

Hans was quite startled and fell to thinking.

21

Then he asked timidly: "Do you still have the text?"

The fellow pulled out his booklet and they went over the text word by word, sentence by sentence. The Göppingen candidate seemed to be a whiz in Latin; at least twice he used grammatical terms Hans had not heard of.

"And what do we have tomorrow?"

"Greek and German composition."

Then Hans was asked how many candidates his school had sent.

"Just myself."

"Ouch. There are twelve of us here from Göppingen. Three really bright guys who are expected to place among the top ten. Last year the fellow who came in first was from Göppingen too. Are you going on to Gymnasium if you fail?"

This was something Hans had never discussed with anyone.

"I have no idea. . . . No, I don't think so."

"Really? I'll keep on studying no matter what happens, even if I fail now. My mother will let me go to school in Ulm."

This revelation impressed Hans immensely. Those twelve candidates from Göppingen and the three really bright ones did not make him feel any easier either. It didn't look as if he stood much of a chance.

At home he sat down and took one last look at the verbs. He had not been worried about Latin, he had been sure of himself in that field. But Greek was a different matter altogether. He certainly liked it, but he was enthusiastic about it only when it came to reading. Xenophon especially was so beautiful and fluent and fresh. It sounded light, vigorous and free-spirited, and was easy to understand. But as soon as it became a question of grammar, or of translating from German into Greek, he seemed to enter a maze of contradictory rules and forms and was as awed by the unfamiliar language as he had been during his very first Greek lesson when he had not even known the alphabet.

The Greek text the next day was fairly long and by no means easy. The German composition theme was so tricky that it could be easily misunderstood. His pen-nib was not a good one and he ruined two sheets before he could make a fair copy of the Greek. During the German composition, a desk neighbor had the gall to slip him a note with questions and jab him repeatedly in the ribs demanding the answers. Any communication with neighbors was of course strictly prohibited and an infraction meant exclusion from the examination. Trembling with fear, Hans wrote: "Leave me alone," and turned his back on the fellow. And it was so hot. Even the supervisor who walked up and down the room without resting for a moment passed his handkerchief over his face several times. Hans sweated in his thick confirmation suit, got a headache and finally turned in his examination booklet. He was far from happy, and certain that it was full of mistakes. Most likely he had reached the end of the line as far as the examination was concerned.

He did not say a word at lunch, shrugged off all questions and made the sour face of a delinquent. His aunt tried to console him but his father became wrought up and began to annoy him. After the meal, he took the boy into another room and tried to delve into the exam once more.

"It went badly," Hans insisted.

"Why didn't you pay more attention? You could have pulled yourself together, by God!"

Hans remained silent, but when his father began to curse, he blushed and said: "You don't understand anything about Greek."

The worst of it was that he had an oral at two o'clock. This he dreaded more than all the other tests combined. Walking through the hot city streets on his way to the afternoon test, he began to feel quite ill. He could hardly see straight with misery, fright and dizziness.

For ten minutes he sat facing three gentlemen across a wide green table, translated a few Latin sentences, and answered their questions. For another ten minutes he sat in front of three other gentlemen, translated from the Greek, and answered another set of questions. At the end they asked him if he knew an irregularly formed aorist, but he didn't.

"You can go now. There's the door, to your right."

He got up, but at the door he remembered the aorist. He stopped.

"Go ahead," they called to him. "Go ahead. Or aren't you feeling well?"

"No, but the aorist just came back to me."

He shouted the answer into the room, saw one of the gentlemen break out in laughter, and rushed with a burning face out of the room. Then he tried to recollect the questions and his answers, but everything was in a big muddle. Time and again the sight of the wide green table with the three serious old gentlemen in frock coats flashed through his mind, the open book, his hand trembling on top of it. My God, his answers must really have been quite something!

As he walked through the streets, he felt as if he had been in the city for weeks and would never be able to leave it. His father's garden at home, the mountains blue with fir trees, the fishing holes by the river seemed like something experienced ages ago. Oh, if he could only go home now. There was no sense staying anyway, he'd flunked the examination for sure.

He bought himself a sweet roll and killed the afternoon wandering through the streets, so he wouldn't have to face his father. When he finally came home they were upset, and because he looked so worn out and miserable, they gave him a bowl of broth and sent him to bed. The next morning he would have tests in mathematics and religion, then he could return home to the village.

Everything went quite well in the morning. Hans regarded it as bitter irony that he should succeed in everything on this day after having had such bad luck in his major subjects the day before. No matter, all he really wanted was to get back home.

"The exams are over, now I can leave," he announced to his aunt.

His father wanted to stay for the day and drive to Cannstatt and have coffee in the garden of the spa there. But Hans implored him so vehemently that his father permitted him to leave that very day. He was escorted to the train, given his ticket, a kiss from his aunt and something to eat. Now he traveled exhausted, his mind a blank, through the green hill country. Only when he saw the mountain covered with dark fir trees did a feeling of joy and relief come over the boy. He looked forward to seeing Anna, the maid, and his little room, the principal, the familiar low-ceilinged schoolroom and just anything.

Fortunately no nosy acquaintances were at the station and he was able to hurry home with his little valise without anyone seeing him.

"Was it good in Stuttgart?" asked Anna.

"Good? How can an examination be good? I'm just glad to be home. Father'll be back tomorrow."

He drank a bowl of fresh milk, fetched his bathing trunks that hung in front of the window, and ran off, though not to the meadow where all the others went swimming.

He walked far out of town to the "scale" where the water flowed slowly and deeply between high bushes. There he undressed, tested the water first with his hand and then his foot, shuddered a moment and then plunged headfirst into the cool river. Swimming slowly against the weak current, he sensed himself shedding the sweat and fear of the last days. He swam more quickly, rested, swam on and felt enveloped by a pleasant fatigue and coolness. Floating on his back he let himself drift down river again, listened to the delicate humming of the evening flies swarming about in golden circles, watched swallows slice through a sky tinted pink by the sun which had set behind the mountains. After he had dressed and ambled dreamily home, the valley was filled with shadows.

He walked past Sackmann, the shopkeeper's garden. As a little boy he'd stolen a few unripe plums there once with a few friends. He walked past Kirchner's timber yard. White fir-beams lay about under which he used to find worms for bait. Then he passed the house of Inspector Gessler on whose daughter, Emma, he'd had such a crush two years ago when they went ice-skating. She was the most delicate and best-dressed schoolgirl in town, she was his age, and there had been a time when he had longed for nothing so much as to speak to her or take her hand just once. But it had never come to much, he had been too shy. She attended a boarding school now and he hardly remembered what she looked like. All these incidents from his boyhood came back to him as from a great distance, yet so vividly that they seemed imbued with promise—like nothing he had experienced since. Those had been the days when he sat in Naschold's doorway where Liese peeled potatoes, listening to her stories; when, early on Sunday with rolled-up pants and a guilty conscience, he had gone to the dam looking for crayfish or to steal minnows from the traps, only to get a thrashing in his Sunday clothes from his father afterwards. There had been such a profusion of puzzling people and things—he had not given them any thought for such a long time. The cobbler with a twisted neck, and Strohmeyer who (everyone said) had poisoned his wife, and the adventurous "Herr" Beck, who had wandered all over the province with a walking stick and rucksack and who was addressed as "Herr" because he had once been wealthy and owned four horses and a carriage. Hans knew little more than their names and sensed dimly that this obscure small world of lanes and valleys was lost to him without ever having been replaced by something lively or worth experiencing.

Because he still had leave from school that day, he slept well into the morning and enjoyed his freedom. At noon he met his father at the station. His father still babbled blissfully about all his Stuttgart experiences.

"I'll give you anything you wish if you've passed," he said happily. "Give it some thought."

28

"No, no," sighed the boy. "I'm sure I failed."

"Nonsense, what's the matter with you? Tell me what you want before I change my mind."

"I'd like to be able to go fishing again during vacation."

"Fine. You can if you pass."

Next day, a Sunday, there was a thunderstorm and downpour and Hans sat for hours in his room, thinking and reading. Once more he reviewed what he had accomplished in Stuttgart and again reached the conclusion that he'd had rotten luck and could have done much better. Anyway, he certainly hadn't done well enough to pass. That stupid headache! Gradually he began to feel oppressed by a growing dread, and finally he went to see his father, profoundly worried.

"Father—"

"What's the matter?"

"I'd like to ask something. About the wish. I'd rather not go fishing."

"Why do you bring that up again now?"

"Because I . . . I wanted to ask whether I couldn't . . ."

"Out with it. What a farce. What is it?"

"Whether I could go to secondary school if I didn't pass?"

Herr Giebenrath was left speechless.

"What? Secondary school?" he exploded. "Go to secondary school? Who put that scheme into your head?"

"No one, I just thought . . ."

Deathly fear stood written all over his face but the father didn't notice.

"Off with you, off," he said with an unhappy laugh. "What extravagant notions. You seem to think I'm a bank president."

He dismissed the matter so decisively that Hans gave up and went outside in despair.

"What a kid that is," he heard his father grumbling behind him. "It's unbelievable, now he wants to go to secondary school. Give them an inch and . . ."

For half an hour Hans sat on the window sill, stared at the freshly polished floor boards and tried to imagine what it would be like if he was unable to attend the academy or secondary school and continue his studies. He would be apprenticed to some cheesy shop or become a clerk in an office and his entire life he would be one of the ordinary poor people, whom he despised and wanted to surpass. His handsome, intelligent schoolboy's face twisted into an ugly grimace filled with anger and suffering. In a fury he leapt up, spat out, grabbed the Latin anthology lying by his side and with all his strength tossed it against the wall. Then he ran out into the rain.

Monday morning he went to school.

"How is everything?" asked the principal, shaking his hand. "I thought you would come to see me yesterday. How did the examination go?"

Hans lowered his head.

"Well, what is it? Didn't you do well?"

"I guess I did, yes."

"Just be patient," the old man soothed him. "Presumably we'll have the results from Stuttgart this morning."

The morning seemed endless. The results did not come, and by lunchtime Hans could hardly swallow, he was so close to sobbing out loud.

When he entered the classroom at two in the afternoon the teacher was there.

"Hans Giebenrath!" he exclaimed loudly.

Hans stepped forward. The teacher shook his hand.

"My congratulations. You came in second in the state examination."

A solemn hush settled over the classroom, the door opened and the principal entered.

"My congratulations. Well, what do you say now?"

The boy seemed totally paralyzed with surprise and joy.

"Well, haven't you anything to say?"

"If I'd known that," he blurted out, "I could have come in first."

"Well, you can go home now," said the principal, "and tell your father the good news. No need to come back to school. Vacation starts in eight days anyway."

In a daze, the boy emerged into the street. He saw the linden trees and the marketplace lying in the sunlight. Everything was as usual and yet more beautiful. By God, he had passed! And he'd come in *second*. When the first wave of joy had waned, a deep gratitude filled him. Now he could look the pastor in the eye. Now he could study, now he need not fear the drudgery of a grocery store or an office.

And he could go fishing again. His father stood in the doorway as he came home.

"What's up?" he asked lightly.

"Nothing much. They've dismissed me from school."

"What? But why?"

"Because I'm an academician now."

"Well, I'll be damned, did you pass?"

Hans nodded.

"How well?"

"I came in second."

That was more than the old man had expected. He did not know what to say, kept patting his son on the shoulder, laughed and shook his head back and forth. Then he opened his mouth as if to say something, but just kept shaking his head.

"I'll be damned," he exclaimed once more, and again, "I'll be damned."

Hans rushed into the house, up the stairs to the loft, tore open the wall closet, rummaged around in it, pulled out a variety of boxes and rolled-up tackle-line and pieces of cork. It was his fishing gear. All he had to do now was cut himself a good rod. He went downstairs to his father.

"Father, can I borrow your hunting knife?"

"What for?"

"To cut myself a rod."

His father reached into his pocket. "There you are," he said with a beaming smile, "there are two marks. Go buy yourself a knife of your own. But go to the cutler's, not to Hanfried."

Now everything was done at top speed. The cutler inquired how he had done in the examination, listened to the good news and found a particularly good knife for Hans. Down river, below the bridge to Brühel, stood beautiful, slim alder and hazel bushes. There, after making a careful choice, he cut himself a perfect, tough and springy rod and hurried home with it.

His face flushed and with glowing eyes, he sat down to the cheerful task of preparing his rod; he liked this almost as much as the fishing itself. He spent an entire afternoon and evening at the job. The white and brown lines were sorted, painstakingly inspected, repaired and freed of many old knots and tangles. Cork floats and quills of all shapes and sizes were tested and freshly cut, little pieces of lead were hammered into pellets and provided with notches for weighting the lines. Then he busied himself with the hooks—he had a small supply left over. He fastened them, some on four-ply black thread, others on a gut-string, the rest on horsehair that had been twisted together. Toward midnight everything was ready. Hans was certain he would not be bored during the long seven weeks of vacation, for he could spend entire days alone with his fishing rod by the river.

Chapter Two

THAT'S HOW SUMMER vacations should be! A gentian-blue sky above the hills, one brilliant hot day after the other for weeks on end, punctuated only by brief and violent thundershowers. The river, though it flowed over sandstone cliffs, through gorges and forests, was so warm you could take a dip in it even late in the afternoon. All around town you smelled the fragrance of hay and flowers, and the few narrow strips of land on which wheat was grown turned yellow and russet; white, hemlock-like weeds shot up high and bloomed luxuriant along the brooks, their white blossoms always covered by an umbrella-like smudge of tiny insects, and they had stalks from which you could cut yourself flutes and pipes. Long rows of wooly and majestic mullein displayed themselves along the forest edges; willow catkin and purple loosestrife swayed on their tough slender stalks, bathing entire slopes violet. Inside the forest itself, under the spruce trees, stood solemn and beautiful and strange the high, steep, red foxglove with its broad, fibrous, silvery root leaves, the strong stalk and the high rows of beautiful red throat-shaped blossoms. Next to them all kinds of mushrooms: the shiny red fly-agaric, the fat and fleshy ordinary mushroom, the red tangled coral-mushroom, the curiously colorless and sickly-looking Pine Bird's Nest. On the many heather-covered banks between the forest and the fields there blazed the tough, fiery-yellow broom, then came long strips of lilac-red heather followed by the fields themselves, most of them ready for the second mowing, overgrown with a profusion of cardamine, campions, meadow sage, knapweed. The woods resounded with the ceaseless chirping and singing of the finches. In the pine forest fox-red squirrels leapt from tree to tree; along ridges, walls and dry ditches green lizards sunned themselves, and over the meadows you could hear the endless ululations, the untiring trumpeting of the cicadas.

The town made a very bucolic impression at this time of year. There were hay wagons about; the scent of grass and clanging of scythes filled streets and air. If there hadn't been two factories, you would have thought you were in a rural village.

Early in the morning of his first day of vacation, Hans stood impatiently in the kitchen waiting for his coffee practically before Anna had had time to get out of bed. He helped lay the fire, fetched bread from the baker, quickly gulped down coffee cooled with fresh milk, stuffed some bread into his pocket and rushed off. At the upper railroad embankment he took a round tin box out of his pants pocket and busied himself catching grasshoppers. The train passed—not in a great swoosh but at a comfortable pace because of a steep incline —with all its windows open and just a handful of passengers, a long banner of smoke and steam trailing behind. Hans gazed after it, watching the smoke dissolve and disappear in the sunny air. He inhaled deeply as if he wanted to make up doubly for all the time he had lost and to be once more a carefree, uninhibited boy.

His heart trembled with delight and the eagerness of the hunt as he carried his box full of grasshoppers and the new rod across the bridge and through the gardens in back to the "horse trough," the deepest part of the river. There was a spot where, if you leaned against a willow, you could fish more comfortably and with fewer interruptions than anywhere else. He unwound his line, tied the little lead pellets to it, ruthlessly impaled a plump grasshopper and cast with a broad sweep toward the middle of the river. The old, well-known game began: little minnows swarmed in swirling shoals around the bait, trying to tear it off the hook. Soon the bait had been nibbled away and it was a second grasshopper's turn, and a third, and fourth and fifth. He fastened them more and more carefully on his hook, finally weighted the line down with a second pellet, and now the first genuine fish tested the bait. He nudged it a little, let it go, then pulled at it again. Now the fish bit. A good fisherman feels the jerk through the line and rod in his fingers. Then Hans gave an artful twist and began to draw in his line very carefully. The fish was properly hooked and when it became visible Hans recognized it as a rudd. You recognize rudds at once by the broad belly which shimmers white-yellow, the triangular head, but most of all by the beautiful fleshy pink of their ventral fins. How much would it weigh? But before he even had a chance to guess its weight, the fish made a desperate leap, thrashed about the surface and escaped. You could still see it make three or four turns in the water, then disappear like a silver streak into the depths. It had not been a proper bite after all.

The excitement, the passionate concentration of the hunt had now taken hold of Hans. His eyes did not once waver from the thin brown line where it entered the water; his cheeks were flushed, his movements short, swift and sure. A second rudd bit and was landed, then a carp almost too small to be worth the trouble; then, one after the other, three gudgeons. The gudgeons made him particularly happy because his father liked them. They are meaty, have tiny scales, a thick head and an odd-looking white beard, small eyes and a slender tail. Their color is mixed brown and gray and on land shades to steel-blue.

In the meantime the sun had risen higher. The foam at the upper dam glistened white as snow, warm air trembled above the water, and if you looked up you could see a few blindingly white clouds the size of your palm. It became hot. Nothing expresses the heat of a midsummer day more emphatically than a few clouds that seem to stand still and white halfway between the blue and the earth, clouds so saturated with light you cannot bear to look at them for long. If it were not for these clouds you would not realize how hot it was. Neither the blue sky nor the glistening mirror of the river would tell you, but as soon as you see a few foamy white, compact, noonday sailors you suddenly feel the sun burn, look for a shadow and wipe the sweat off your brow.

Hans found his attention slipping. He was a little tired, and besides, the chances of catching anything around noon are poor. The whitefish, even the oldest and biggest of them, surface at this time for a sunbath. Dreamily they swim upstream in large dark shoals, close to the surface, occasionally startled without visible cause. They refuse to bite during these hours.

He slung his line over a willow branch into the water, sat down and gazed into the green river. The fish rose slowly. One dark back after the other broke the surface—calm processions swimming lazily, drawn upward, enchanted by the warmth. No doubt about how well they felt! Hans slipped his boots off and dangled his feet into the lukewarm water. He inspected his catch swimming in a big bucket, softly splashing every so often. How beautiful they were! White, brown, green, silver, wangold, blue and other colors glistened on the scales and fins with every move.

It was very quiet. You could barely hear the wagons rumbling as they crossed the bridge and the splash of the mill wheel was indistinct from where he sat. Only the unceasing sound of water pouring over the dam and washing drowsily past the raft timbers.

Greek, Latin, grammar, style, math and learning by rote, the whole torturous process of a long, restless and hectic year quietly sank away in the warmth of this sleepy hour. Hans had a slight headache but it was not as painful as usual. He watched the foam break into spray at the weir, glanced at the line and the bucket beside him with the fish he'd caught. It was all so delicious! Intermittently he would remember that he had passed the examination and come in second. Then he would slap his naked feet into the water, stick both hands into his pants pockets and begin whistling a song. He could not really whistle properly. This had been a sore point with him for a long time and had made him the butt of many of his schoolmates' jokes. He was only able to whistle softly and only through his teeth but it was good enough for his purpose and anyway no one could overhear him now. The others were still in school and had a geography lesson.

Only he was free. He had outstripped them,

they were now below him. They had pestered him because he had made friends only with August and never really enjoyed their rough-and-ready games and pleasures. Well, now they could go to hell, the oafs, the fatheads. He despised them so thoroughly he stopped whistling for a moment just to contort his mouth in disgust. Then he wound in his line and had to laugh, for there was not a trace of bait on the hook. He freed the remaining grasshoppers and they crawled shakily into the short grass. In the nearby tannery the workers were having their lunchbreak; it was time for him to go eat, too.

Hardly a word was said at table.

"Did you catch anything?" asked his father.

"Five of them."

"Really? Just you make sure you don't catch the old one, or there won't be any young ones later on."

With this the conversation lapsed. It was so warm out. It was a shame you couldn't go swimming right after a meal. Why was that? It was supposed to be harmful. Nonsense! Hans knew better than that. Though it was forbidden, he'd done it often enough. But he wouldn't do it again now, he was too mature for such pranks. At the examination they had even addressed him as "Mister."

Then again, it was not bad to lie for an hour in the garden, under the spruce. It was cool in the shadows and you could read a book or observe the butterflies. So he lay there until two o'clock and

nearly fell asleep. But now to the swimming hole!
Only a few small boys were in the meadow. The
bigger ones were still in school and Hans didn't
begrudge them their fate. He undressed slowly
and then slid into the water. He knew how to
make the best of coolness and of warmth. Alter-
nately he would swim, dive and splash about, then
lie face down on the river bank and feel the sun
dry his skin. The little boys kept their distance.
Indeed, he had become a celebrity, and besides,
he looked so different from the rest. His handsome head sat on a thin tanned neck, and there
was an intelligent and superior look to his face.
Also he was quite skinny, with thin limbs and a
fragile, delicate build. You could count his ribs
both in front and back.

He divided the afternoon almost evenly between sunbathing and going for brief swims. Then
at about four most of his classmates came running
noisily and in a great rush.

"Hey, Giebenrath, leading the easy life, are
you?"

He stretched out comfortably. "No complaints,
no complaints."

"When are you leaving for the academy?"

"Not until September. I'm on vacation until
then."

He let them envy him. He wasn't bothered in
the least when he heard them joking about him in
the background. Someone intoned a mocking verse:

41

"If I just had it like her,
Like Schulze's Elizabeth,
Who spends all day in bed—
But I don't."

He merely laughed. Meantime the boys undressed. One of them jumped straight into the water; others, more cautious, cooled off first; some even lay down in the grass to rest. A boy who was about to chicken out altogether was pushed into the water from behind. They chased each other, running and swimming and splashing those taking sun baths. The splashing and shrieking was terrific. The whole breadth of the river glistened with white shining bodies.

Hans left after another hour had passed. The warm hours of the afternoon when the fish bite were drawing near. Until supper he fished from the bridge and caught next to nothing. The fish were made for his hook; every few seconds the bait had been devoured but they avoided the barb. He had baited it with cherries. Evidently they were too large and soft and so he decided to give it another try later on.

At supper he heard that many relatives had stopped by to congratulate him. He was also given the local weekly. Under the heading *Official Notice* he could read the following text:

"This year our town sent only one candidate to the state examination for the theological academy, Hans Giebenrath. To our gratification we have just been informed that Hans Giebenrath passed the examination and came in second."

He folded the sheet and stuck it in his back pocket, not saying anything, but he was almost ready to burst with pride and joy. Afterwards he went back to fish. He took a few pieces of cheese along because fish like it and it is visible to them in the dusk. However, he left the rod behind and only took the line. He preferred to fish this way, just the line without rod and float, so that the tackle consists of just line and hook. Fishing became a little more strenuous but much more fun. You had complete control over every movement of the bait, felt every touch and nibble, and by observing the twitch of the line you could follow the fish as if it were actually in front of your eyes. Of course you have to know what you are doing when you fish like this, your fingers must be quick; you have to be as alert as a spy.

Dusk fell early in the winding narrows of this deeply indented river valley. The water lay tranquilly under the bridge and lights had been turned on at one of the mills downstream. Loud talk and singing could be heard from the bridges and narrow streets. The air was a little muggy. In the river a dark fish leaped into the air with a sharp splash every few seconds. Fish are remarkably excited on evenings like this—they zigzag back and forth, leap into the air, collide with the line and hurl themselves blindly at the bait. When the last piece of cheese was gone Hans had caught four small carp. He decided to bring them to the pastor in the morning.

A warm breeze was blowing down-valley. Though the sky was still pale it was rapidly getting dark. Of the entire town only the church tower and the roof of the castle were visible jutting like black silhouettes into the pale sky. Somewhere at a great distance there was a thunderstorm—you could hear occasional muffled rumbling.

When Hans went to bed at ten o'clock he was pleasurably tired in mind and limb as he had not been for a long time. A series of beautiful, carefree summer days stretched out before him, calm and alluring, days he would idle away swimming, fishing, dreaming. Only one thing irked him: he had not come in *first* in the examination.

Very early next morning Hans stood in the foyer of the pastorage to deliver his carp. The pastor emerged from his study.

"Oh, Giebenrath. Good morning and my congratulations. What do you have there?"

"Just a few fish I caught yesterday."

"Well, look at that! Thank you, but now come inside."

Hans stepped into the familiar study. It actually did not look like a pastor's room. It neither smelled of the earth of potted plants nor of tobacco. The substantial library consisted mostly of new, freshly varnished and gilded spines, not of the worn, bent, worm-eaten or mildewed volumes you usually find in pastors' libraries. If you inspected them closely you detected from the titles of the well-arranged volumes that a modern spirit ruled here, different from that of the old-fashioned, honorable gentlemen of the previous generation. The esteemed showpieces of the pastor's library, volumes by Bengel, Otinger, Steinhofer, plus all the collections of devout songs which Mörike treats so affectionately in the *Turmhahn*, were missing or lacked prominence among the mass of modern works. All in all, the lectern, the large desk and the periodical holders lent the room a dignified, learned air. You received the impression that much work was accomplished here, and that was indeed the case. Of course, less effort was devoted to sermons, catechism and Bible hours than to research and articles for learned journals and preparatory studies for the pastor's own books. Vague mysticism and premonition-filled longing were banned, as was the "theology of the heart," which goes out to the thirsting souls of the people with love and charity, crossing the gulf of science. Instead Biblical criticism and a zealous search for the historical Christ were pursued.

For the first time in his life Hans was allowed to sit on the little leather sofa between the lectern and the window. The pastor was more than friendly. In a most comradely fashion he told Hans about the academy and how one lived and studied there.

"The most important new experience that you

will have there is the introduction to the Greek of the New Testament," he said at the end. "This will open up an entirely new world to you, rich in work and pleasure. At first you will find the language difficult because it is no longer the Attic Greek with which you are familiar but a new idiom, created by a different spirit."

Hans listened attentively and proudly felt himself drawing nearer to true science.

"The academic introduction into this new world," the pastor continued, "will of course rob it of some of its magic. The study of Hebrew may also make rather one-sided demands on you at first. If you like, we can make a small beginning during your vacation. You'll be glad once you get to the academy to have time and energy left over for other things. We could read a few chapters of Luke together, and you would pick up the language almost unintentionally. I can lend you a dictionary. You would have to spend an hour or two a day at most. But no more than that because, more than anything else, you should be able to enjoy the period of relaxation you so highly deserve. It's only a suggestion of course, the last thing I want to do is spoil your holiday."

Hans of course agreed to the proposal. Although this Luke lesson looked to him like a small cloud in the promising blue vacation sky, he was too ashamed to say no. And to learn a new language, just like that, during his vacation certainly was more like pleasure than work. In any case, he

46

was somewhat anxious about the many new things he would have to learn at the academy, especially Hebrew.

So he was not displeased when he left the pastor and made his way up the path lined with larches to the forest. The slight doubt he had felt had passed and the more he thought about the proposition the more acceptable it seemed to him. For he was aware that in the academy he would have to be even more ambitious if he wanted to outstrip his new fellow students. Why did he want to surpass them actually? He didn't really know himself. For three years now he had been the object of special attention. The teachers, the pastor, his father and particularly the principal had egged and urged him on and had never let him catch his breath. All these years from grade to grade he had been first in his class, until it had gradually become a matter of pride for him to come in first and brook no rivals. At least his stupid fear of the state examination was behind him.

Still, to be on vacation was actually the best thing in the world. How unusually beautiful the forest was in the morning without anyone walking through it but him, column after column of spruce, a vast hall with a blue-green vault. There was little real underbrush, only an occasional raspberry thicket and a broad felt of moss dotted with bilberries and heather. The dew had evaporated. Between the bolt-straight trunks there hovered a mugginess characteristic of forests in the morning, a mixture compounded of the sun's warmth, mist, the smell of moss and resin, fir needles and mushrooms which caresses all one's senses like a gentle anesthetic. Hans flung himself on the moss, picked the generous bilberry bushes clean, heard here and there a woodpecker hammer against a tree trunk and the call of the envious cuckoo. The spotless deep blue sky was visible between the blackish spruce crowns and in the distance thousands upon thousands of vertical columns crowded together into a single solemn brown wall. Here and there a yellow spot of sun gleamed warm, strewn opulently on the moss.

Actually Hans had wanted to go on a long ramble, at least as far as Lützeler Hof or the crocus meadow. Now he reclined in the moss, ate bilberries and gazed listlessly into the air. He began to wonder why he was so tired. Formerly a walk of three or four hours had been a lark. Now he decided to pull himself together and to cover a good stretch of his planned excursion. He walked a few hundred steps. Then he lay down in the moss again—he hardly knew himself how it had happened, but he just lay there, his glance roving distractedly among the trunks and crowns and along the green floor. He wondered why this air made him so drowsy.

When he came home around noon he had a headache again. His eyes too hurt him—the sun had been blinding along the forest path. Half the afternoon, he sat moodily around the house; only when he went swimming did he revive. Then it was time to go see the pastor.

Shoemaker Flaig, sitting on his three-legged stool by the window, caught sight of him as he passed and asked him in.

"Where are you off to, son? Where have you been keeping yourself these days?"

"I have to go see the pastor."

"You're still going? But isn't the examination over?"

"Yes, it is. We're working on something else now. The New Testament. That was written in Greek too, but in an entirely different Greek from that which I have learned. That's what I'm supposed to learn now."

The shoemaker pushed his cap back onto his neck and screwed his forehead into deep quizzical furrows. Then he gave a deep sigh.

"Hans," he said gently, "I want to tell you something. I've laid low on account of the exam, but now I have to warn you. You should know that the pastor is an unbeliever. He will try to tell you that the Scriptures are false, and once you've read through the New Testament with him you'll have lost your faith and you won't know how."

"But, Master Flaig, it's just a question of Greek. I'll have to learn it anyway once I enter the academy."

"That's what you say. But it's an entirely dif-

49

ferent matter if you study the Bible under devout and conscientious teachers than with someone who does not believe in God."

"Yes, but no one really knows, do they, whether he believes or doesn't?"

"Oh yes, Hans, unfortunately we do know."

"But what should I do? It's all arranged that I go see him."

"Then you'll have to go, naturally. But when he says things like the Bible was written by human beings and not inspired by the Holy Ghost, then come see me and we'll discuss it. Would you like that?"

"Yes, Master Flaig, but I'm sure it won't be as bad as all that."

"You'll see. Remember what I said."

The pastor had not come home yet and Hans had to wait for him in his study. While looking at the gilded titles, he could not help thinking of what the shoemaker had said. He had heard similar comments about the pastor and modern theology several times before. But now for the first time he felt himself becoming involved, interested in these matters. They seemed by no means as important and awful to him as to the shoemaker. On the contrary, he sensed the possibility of coming near to the heart of old, great mysteries. In his early school years the questions of God's immanence, the abode of human souls after the death of the body, and the nature of the devil and hell had driven him to fantastic speculations. Yet these interests had subsided again during those last strict hard-working years, and his orthodox, unquestioning Christianity had awakened to a genuine personal involvement only occasionally during his conversations with the shoemaker. A smile came over his face when he compared the shoemaker with the pastor. He could not understand how Flaig's sturdy faith had grown through so many trying years. If Flaig was intelligent, he was also an unimaginative, one-sided man whom many people mocked because of his evangelizing. At meetings of the Pietists he performed the role of stern if brotherly judge, and as a formidable exponent of Holy Scripture he also conducted inspirational sessions in the nearby villages, but otherwise he was just an ordinary craftsman with all the limitations of his kind. The pastor, on the other hand, was not only a clever and eloquent man and preacher but also an assiduous and careful scholar. Hans gazed with awe at the rows of books.

The pastor came soon, changed his outdoor coat for a black house jacket, handed his pupil the Greek text of Luke and asked him to read it. This was quite different from what the Latin lessons had been like. They read just a few sentences, translating them faithfully word by word, then his teacher developed from seemingly unpromising examples a clever and convincing demonstration of the spirit peculiar to this language, and discussed how and at what time the book came to be written. In a single hour he introduced Hans to an entirely new approach to learning and reading. Hans received an intimation of what tasks and puzzles lay hidden in each line and word, how thousands of scholars and investigators had expended their efforts since the earliest times to unravel these questions, and it seemed to him that he was being accepted into the ranks of these truth-seekers this very hour.

The pastor lent him a dictionary and a grammar and he continued to work for the rest of the evening. Now he began to realize across how many mountains of work and knowledge the path to true science leads and he was prepared to hack his way through without taking any short cuts. Shoemaker Flaig, for the time being, slipped his mind.

For a few days this new revelation absorbed him completely. Each evening he visited the pastor and every day true scholarship seemed more beautiful, more difficult, more worthwhile. Early in the morning he went fishing, in the afternoon to the swimming hole; otherwise he stayed in the house. His ambition, diminished during the anxiety and triumph of the examination, had reawakened and would not let him retreat. Simultaneously he again felt that peculiar sensation in his head, felt so often during the last months, which was not precisely a pain but a hurried, triumphant pulsation of hectically excited energies, an impetuous desire to advance. Afterwards, of course, he would come down with a headache, but as long as this febrile state lasted, his reading and work moved forward at a lightning pace and he could read with ease the most difficult construction in Xenophon, one which usually took him fifteen minutes. Then he hardly needed a dictionary but flew with sharpened understanding across the most difficult passages quickly and happily. This heightened activity and thirst for knowledge also coincided with a proud sense of self-esteem, as though school and teachers and the years of study lay far behind him and as though he were already taking his own path toward the heights of knowledge and achievement.

All this came over him again, and again he slept fitfully and dreamed with a peculiar clarity. Thus, when he awoke in the night with a slight headache and could not fall back to sleep, he was overwhelmed by an impatience to forge ahead and by a great pride when he considered how far ahead of his companions he was and how the teacher and the principal had treated him with a kind of respect, admiration even.

The principal had taken genuine satisfaction in guiding and observing the growth of this ambition which he himself had kindled. It is wrong to say that schoolmasters lack heart and are dried-up, soulless pedants! No, by no means. When a child's talent which he has sought to kindle suddenly bursts forth, when the boy puts aside his wooden sword, slingshot, bow-and-arrow and other childish games, when he begins to forge ahead, when the seriousness of the work begins to transform the rough-neck into a delicate, serious and an almost ascetic creature, when his face takes on an intelligent, deeper and more purposeful expression—then a teacher's heart laughs with happiness and pride. It is his duty and responsibility to control the raw energies and desires of his charges and replace them with calmer, more moderate ideals. What would many happy citizens and trustworthy officials have become but unruly, stormy innovators and dreamers of useless dreams, if not for the effort of their schools? In young beings there is something wild, ungovernable, uncultured which first has to be tamed. It is like a dangerous flame that has to be controlled or it will destroy. Natural man is unpredictable, opaque, dangerous, like a torrent cascading out of uncharted mountains. At the start, his soul is a jungle without paths or order. And, like a jungle, it must first be cleared and its growth thwarted. Thus it is the school's task to subdue and control man with force and make him a useful member of society, to kindle those qualities in him whose development will bring him to triumphant completion.

How well little Giebenrath had come along! He'd given up playing games and running about almost of his own accord, he no longer burst out in stupid laughter during lectures, and he had even let himself be persuaded to abandon his gardening, his rabbits and silly fishing.

One fine evening the principal himself came to

visit the Giebenraths. After he had spent a few polite minutes with the flattered father, he stepped into Hans' room only to find the boy sitting in front of his Luke. He greeted him in a friendly fashion.

"That's good of you, Giebenrath, already back at work! But why don't you ever show your face? I've been expecting you every day."

"I would have come," Hans excused himself, "but I wanted to bring at least one good fish along."

"Fish, what kind of fish?"

"Just a carp or something like that."

"Oh, I see. You're going fishing again."

"Yes, just a little. Father allowed me to."

"Well well. Are you enjoying it?"

"Yes, of course."

"Fine, very fine. You certainly deserve a vacation. So you probably don't want to learn anything on the side."

"But of course I do, naturally."

The principal took a few deep breaths, stroked his thin beard once and sat down on a chair.

"Look, Hans," he began. "Things are like this. It has been known for a long time that a good examination is frequently followed by a sudden letdown. At the academy you will have to cope with several entirely new subjects. There are always a number of students who prepare themselves for these tasks during the vacation—especially those students who have done less well in the examination. And these students then suddenly spurt forward at the expense of those who have rested on their laurels."

He gave another sigh.

"You had an easy time of it here in school but at the academy you'll face stiffer competition. Your fellow students will all be talented and hard-working and you won't be able to surpass them with the same ease. You understand what I mean, don't you?"

"Oh, yes."

"Now I wanted to suggest that you work a little in advance during the vacation. Of course, with moderation. I thought that one or two hours a day would be just about right. If you didn't work at all, you would certainly lose your momentum and afterwards it takes weeks to get the wind back in your sails. What do you think?"

"I am ready, sir. If you could be so kind as to . . ."

"Fine. Besides Hebrew, Homer will open up an entirely new world to you. You will read him with twice as much enjoyment and understanding in the academy if we lay the foundation now. The language of Homer, the old Ionian dialect, together with the Homeric prosody is something very special, something singular, and it demands hard study and thoroughness if you want to achieve true appreciation of these works of poetry."

Of course Hans was quite prepared to enter also into this new world and he promised to do his best.

But the better part was still to come. The principal cleared his throat and went on amiably.

"Frankly, it would please me too if you would spend a few hours a day on mathematics. You're not bad at it, yet it has never been your forte until now. In the academy you will be starting on algebra and geometry and you will probably be well advised to take a few preparatory lessons."

"Yes, sir."

"You're always welcome to come see me, you know that. It's a point of honor with me to make something outstanding of you. But you will have to ask your father about the mathematics lessons, since you will have to take private lessons with the professor. Three or four a week perhaps."

"Yes, sir."

No matter how hard Hans applied himself to his math lessons, they gave him little pleasure. After all, it was bitter to have to sit in the professor's study on a muggy afternoon reciting the *a plus b* and *a minus b* while he became more and more tired, his throat dry, with bugs whirring about, and not be at the swimming hole. Something paralyzing and altogether oppressive hovered in the air that bad days could change to inconsolable despair. Hans and mathematics did not get along that well anyway. Yet he was not a student to whom it remained a mystery. Sometimes he would find good, even elegant solutions and he would be pleased. He liked the way mathematics admits nothing fraudulent, no mistakes, no possibility of wandering from the subject to enter treacherous territories adjacent. That was the reason why he liked Latin also: because the language is lucid, unequivocal, devoid of almost all ambiguity. But even when all his mathematical results tallied he did not have a sense of accomplishment. The assignments and lessons seemed to him like wandering on an even highway—you always make progress, every day you learn something you did not know the day before, but you never reach a great height from which you suddenly see new vistas.

The hours with the principal proved livelier, though the pastor knew how to make something more attractive and magnificent out of the New Testament's degenerate Greek than the principal did of the youthfully fresh language of Homer. But in the final analysis it was in Homer that you found irresistible surprises and pleasures lurking behind the first difficulties. Often Hans sat before a mysteriously sonorous verb, trembling with impatience to find in the dictionary the key that would reveal the beauty of the meaning to him.

He had more than enough homework now and often he sat bent stubbornly over some task until late at night. Father Giebenrath regarded all this industry with pride. His cumbersome mind clung to an obscure ideal, shared by many people of limited intellect and venerated with unthinking respect: to let a branch sprout from the main trunk, an extension of himself.

During the last week of vacation the principal and pastor again became noticeably concerned about Hans. They sent the boy on walks, discontinued the lessons and emphasized how important it was for him to enter his new career alert and refreshed.

Hans managed to go fishing a few more times. Often he had headaches, and without really being able to concentrate, he would sit by the bank of the river which now reflected the light blue autumn sky. It was a mystery to him why he had once looked forward so much to the summer vacation. Now he was almost glad it was over so he could leave for the academy where an entirely new course of life and work awaited him. Because it didn't really matter to him any more, he didn't catch many fish. When his father joked about it, he stopped fishing altogether and put his tackle back in the chest in the loft.

Toward the very end of his vacation he remembered that he had neglected shoemaker Flaig for weeks. Even now he literally had to force himself to go see him. It was evening and the master sat at his living-room window, a small child on each knee. Though the window was open, the smell of leather and shoe polish permeated the whole house. Somewhat self-consciously, Hans placed his hand in the callused, broad palm of the master.

"Well, how are things?" he asked. "Did you put in your time with the pastor?"

"Yes, I went every day and I learned a great deal."

"Well, and what?"

"Mainly Greek but all sorts of other things too."

"And you didn't find the time to come see me?"

"I wanted to, Herr Flaig, but somehow it just never worked out. Each day I was at the pastor's for one hour, at the principal's for two hours, and four times a week with the mathematics professor."

"While you were on vacation? What nonsense!"

"I don't know. The teachers thought it was best this way. And learning isn't very difficult for me."

"Maybe so," said Flaig and took the boy's arm. "Nothing is wrong with learning but look at what thin arms you have. You really ought to put on a little weight. Do you still have your headaches?"

"Now and then."

"What nonsense that is, Hans, and a sin besides. At your age one has to get lots of fresh air and exercise and have a good rest. Why do you think you have vacations? Certainly not to sit around your room and go on learning. You're nothing but skin and bones."

Hans laughed.

"Well, you'll fight your way through. But too much is too much. And how did the lessons with the pastor go? What did he say?"

"He said many things but nothing awful. He knows an immense amount."

"Did he never say anything derogatory about the Bible?"

"No, not once."

"I am glad. Because I can tell you this: better to harm your body ten times over than to harm your soul! You want to become a pastor later on and that is a precious and difficult office. Perhaps you are right for it and one day you will be a helper and teacher of souls. I desire that with all my heart and will pray to that end."

He had risen and now placed his hands firmly on the boy's shoulders.

"Take care, Hans, and stay on the good side. May God bless you and keep you, Amen."

The solemnity, the praying, the formal and elevated language were discomforting and embarrassing to the boy. The pastor had said nothing of this sort at their parting.

The last few days passed quickly and restlessly with all the preparations and good-byes Hans had to make. A chest with bed covers, clothes and books had been sent ahead. All that was left to be packed now was his traveling case, and when that was done, father and son set off for Maulbronn one cool morning. Still, it was strange and depressing to be leaving his native place and to move away from his father's house to an alien institution.

Chapter Three

THE LARGE CISTERCIAN monastery of
Maulbronn is situated in the northwest of
the province among wooded hills and small tranquil lakes. Extensive, solidly constructed and well
preserved, the handsome old buildings provide an
attractive abode—they are spectacular both inside
and out, and over the centuries they have formed
a whole with their beautiful, calm, green environs.

If you want to visit the monastery itself, you
step through a picturesque gate in the high wall
onto a broad and peaceful square. A fountain with
running water is at its center, and there are old,
solemn trees. At both sides stand rows of solid
stone houses and in the background is the front
of the main church with a large romanesque
porch, called "The Paradise," of incomparable
gracefulness and enchanting beauty. On the
mighty roof of the church you can see a tower
perched so absurdly small and pointed like a
needle that it seems unbelievable it can bear the
weight of the bell. The transept, itself a beautiful
piece of workmanship, contains as its most precious gem an exquisite wall-chapel. The monks'

refectory with its noble vigorous ribbed vaulting, the oratory, parlor, lay refectory, abbot's house and two churches together form a compact series of buildings. Picturesque walls, bow windows, gardens, a mill and living quarters are like a decorous wreath around the sturdy and ancient buildings. The broad square lies calm and empty and, in its repose, plays with the shadows of the surrounding trees. Only between noon and one o'clock does a fleeting semblance of life pass over it. At that time a group of young people step out of the monastery and, losing themselves in that wide expanse, introduce movement, shouts, conversations, laughter, perhaps a little ball-playing, only to disappear again at the end of that hour behind the wall without leaving a trace. It has occurred to many people while they stood on this square that it would be just the right place for the good life and for happiness, for something lively and gratifying to grow, for mature and good people to think glad thoughts and produce beautiful, cheerful works.

This magnificent monastery, hidden behind hills and woods, has long been reserved for the exclusive use of the students of the Protestant Theological Academy in order that their receptive young spirits will be surrounded by an atmosphere of beauty and peace. Simultaneously the young people are removed from the distracting influence of their towns and families and are preserved from the harmful sight of the active life. So it is possible to let them live under the definite impression that their life's goal consists exclusively of the study of Hebrew and Greek and sundry subjects and to turn the thirst of young souls toward pure and ideal studies and enjoyments. In addition there is the important factor of boarding-school life, the imperative need for self-education, the feeling of belonging together. The grant which makes it possible for the academy students to live and study here free of charge makes very sure that they become imbued with an indelible spirit by which you can recognize them forever after. It is a delicate way of branding them. With the exception of the few wild ones who break free, you can distinguish a Maulbronn student as such for the rest of his life.

Boys who still had a mother when they entered the monastery could think back on those days with touching emotions and gratitude. Hans Giebenrath was not one of these; his mother's absence did not move him in the least, but he was in a position to observe scores of other mothers and this made a curious impression on him.

In the wide corridors with their rows of built-in closets, the so-called dormitories, there stood any number of chests and baskets which the owners and their parents were busy unpacking or stacking with their odds and ends. Everyone had been assigned one of these numbered closets and a numbered bookstall in his study room. Sons and parents knelt on the floor while unpacking. The proctor pranced like a prince among them, freely dispensing advice left and right. Suits were spread out, shirts folded, books stacked, shoes and slippers set out in neat rows. Most of the boys had brought the same major articles because all essentials and the clothes you had to bring were prescribed. Tin washbasins with names scratched into them were unpacked and set up in the washroom; sponges, soap dish, comb and toothbrush next to them. Each boy also brought his own lamp, a can of kerosene and a set of table utensils.

The boys were busy and excited. The fathers smiled, tried to be of some help, cast frequent glances at their pocket watches, but were actually quite bored and looked for excuses to sneak off. The mothers were at the heart of all this activity. Piece by piece they unpacked the suits and under-wear, smoothed out wrinkles, tugged at strings and then, after deciding on the most efficient place-ment of each article, distributed everything as neatly and practically as possible in the closet. Ad-monitions, advice and tender remarks accom-panied this flow of laundry.

"You'll have to take extra care of your shirts. They cost three-fifty apiece."

"You should send the laundry home every four weeks by rail. If you need it in a hurry, send it parcel post. The black hat is for Sundays only."

A comfortably fat woman sat perched on top of a high chest teaching her son the art of sewing on buttons.

"If you become homesick," another mother was saying, "all you have to do is write. And remember, it's not so long until Christmas."

A pretty woman, who was still quite young, took a last look at her son's overstuffed closet and passed her hand lovingly over the piles of linen, jackets and pants. When she was done with this, she began to caress her son, a broad-shouldered, chubby-cheeked boy who was ashamed and tried to fend off his mother. He laughed with embarrassment and then, so as not to appear touched, stuck both hands in his pockets. Their leavetaking seemed to affect the mother much more strongly than her son.

With other students just the opposite was the case. They stared dumbly and helplessly at their busy mothers, and looked as if they would just as soon return home immediately. But the fear of separation and the heightened tenderness and dependency were waging a bitter struggle in all their hearts with their shyness before on-lookers and the first proud signs of their defiant masculinity. Many a boy who wanted nothing more than to burst into tears assumed an artificially careless expression and pretended that none of this mattered to him. The mothers, noticing this, merely smiled.

Most boys, in addition to essentials, had also brought a number of luxury articles. A sackful of apples, a smoked sausage, a basket of baked goods, or something on that order would appear from their chests. Many had brought ice-skates. One skinny, sly-looking fellow drew everyone's attention to himself when he unpacked a whole smoked ham, which he made no attempt to conceal.

It was easy to tell which boys had come straight from home and which had been to boarding school before. Yet even the latter, it was obvious, were excited and tense.

Herr Giebenrath helped his son unpack and set about it in an intelligent and practical fashion. He was done earlier than most other parents and for a while he stood bored and helpless beside Hans. Because everywhere he could see fathers instructing and admonishing, mothers consoling and advising, sons listening in rapt bewilderment, he felt it was only fitting that he too should start Hans out in life with a few golden words of his own. He reflected for a long time and walked in awkward silence beside his son until he suddenly opened fire with a priceless series of pious clichés —which Hans received with dumb amazement. That is, until he saw a nearby deacon break out in an amused smile over his father's speech; then he felt ashamed and drew the speaker aside.

"Agreed, you'll be a credit to the good name of the family? You'll obey your superiors?"

"Of course."

His father fell silent and breathed a sigh of relief. Now he began to get seriously bored. Hans, too, began to feel lost. He looked with perplexed curiosity through the window down into the quiet cloister, where old-fashioned peace and dignity presented a curious contrast to the life upstairs. Then he glanced timidly at his fellow students, not one of whom he knew so far. His Stuttgart examination companion seemed not to have passed, despite his clever Göppingen Latin. At least Hans could see him nowhere around. Without giving it much real thought, Hans inspected his classmates. They were similar in kind and number as their accouterments, and it was easy to tell farmers' sons from city boys, the well-to-do from the poor. The sons of the truly wealthy of course entered the academy only rarely, a fact that let you make an inference about their pride, the deeper wisdom of their parents, or about the innate talent of their children—as the case might be. Nonetheless, a number of professors and higher officials, remembering their own years at the monastery, sent their sons to Maulbronn. Thus you could detect many differences in cloth and cut among the forty-odd black-suited boys. What differentiated them even more clearly from one another were their manners, dialects and bearing. There were lanky fellows from the Black Forest, who had an awkward gait; strutting youths from the Alb; flaxen-haired, wide-mouthed, nimble low-landers with free and easy manners; well-dressed Stuttgarters with pointed shoes and a degenerate—I mean, overly refined—accent. Approximately one-fifth of this select group wore spectacles. One, a slight, almost elegant mother's boy from Stuttgart, wore a stiff felt hat and behaved very politely; he was completely unaware that his unusual decorousness had already laid the ground for future ribbing and bullying from the more daring of his companions.

A more discerning observer could certainly see that this timid little group represented a fair cross section of the youth of the land. Alongside a number of perfectly average faces, those you could spot as earnest drudges even from a distance, you discovered no lack of delicate or sturdy heads behind whose smooth brows presumably existed the still half-asleep dream of a higher life. Perhaps there was among their number one of those clever and stubborn Swabians who would push his way into the mainstream of life and make his ideas, inevitably somewhat dry and narrowly individualistic, the focal point of a new and mighty system. For Swabia supplies the world not only with a fair number of well-prepared theologians but is also graced with a traditional aptitude for philosophical speculation that on more than one occasion has produced noteworthy prophets, not to mention false prophets. And so this productive land, whose politically great tradition has long since passed, still exerts its influence on the world if only through the disciplines of theology and philosophy. You will also find that the people in general are endowed with an age-old taste for beautiful form and for poetry that from time to time has given birth to poets and versifiers of the first order.

Nothing specifically Swabian could be observed in the outward customs and furnishings of the academy in Maulbronn. On the contrary, side by side with the Latin names left over from the time when it had served as a monastery, a number of new classical labels had been affixed. The students' rooms were labeled Forum, Hellas, Athens, Sparta, Acropolis, and the fact that the last and smallest was called Germania seemed to signify a good reason for transforming the Germanic present, if possible, into a Greco-Roman utopia. Yet even these designations were merely decorative—Hebrew names would have been just as scholastically appropriate. As chance would have it, the study called Athens was allotted not to the most articulate and free-spirited boys but to a handful of honest dullards; Sparta did not house warriors or ascetics, but a bunch of happy-go-lucky students who lived off-campus. Hans Giebenrath and nine other pupils were assigned to Hellas.

Contrary to his expectations, a surprisingly strange feeling gripped his heart when he entered this cool, sparse dormitory with the nine others for the first time and lay down in his narrow schoolboy's bed. A big kerosene lamp dangled from the ceiling. You undressed in its red glow. At a quarter to ten it was extinguished by the proctor. There they lay now, one bed beside the other, between every second bed a stool with clothes on it. Along one of the pillars hung the cord which rang the morning bell. Two or three boys who knew each other from home whispered timidly among themselves, but not for long. The others were strangers and each lay slightly depressed and deathly quiet in his bed. You could hear those who were asleep breathing deeply, or one would suddenly lift an arm and the linen rustled. Hans could not fall asleep for a long time. He listened to his neighbors breathing and after a while heard a strangely anxious noise coming from a bed two away from his. Someone was weeping, his blanket pulled over his head, and Hans felt oddly affected by these moans which seemed to reach him from a remote distance. He himself did not feel homesick though he missed his quiet little room. He only felt a slight dread of such an uncertain and novel situation and of his many new companions. It was not yet midnight and everyone in the hall had fallen asleep. The young sleepers lay side by side in their beds, their cheeks pressed into striped pillows: sad and stubborn, easygoing and timid boys vanquished by the same sweet, sound rest and oblivion. Above the old pointed roofs, towers, bow windows, turret, battlements and gothic arcades there rose a pale half-moon and its light lodged in cornices, on window ledges, poured over gothic windows and romanesque gateways and trembled pale-golden in the generous bowl of the cloister's fountain. A few stripes and spots of yellowish light fell through three windows into Hellas' sleeping quarters and kept the slumbering boys neighborly company, just as it had accompanied the dreams of generations of monks.

Next day, in the oratory, the boys were solemnly received into the academy. The teachers were dressed in their frock coats, the headmaster gave an address, the students sat rapt in thought in their chairs and stole an occasional glance at their parents, sitting way in the back. The mothers looked with pensive smiles at their sons; the fathers sat very erect, followed the speech closely and looked serious and determined. Proud and praiseworthy feelings and high hopes swelled in their breasts and it did not occur to a single one of them that this day he was selling his child for a financial advantage. At the end of the ceremony one student after the other was called by name, stepped up and was accepted into the academy with a handshake by the headmaster and was pledged that, provided he behaved himself, he would be duly sheltered and cared for by the state for the rest of his days. It did not occur to any of the boys, nor to their fathers, that all this would perhaps not really be free.

Much more serious and moving was the moment when they took leave of their departing parents. These were now disappearing—some on foot, some by coach, others in any kind of transportation they had been able to arrange in the rush. For a long time handkerchiefs continued to flutter in the mild September air until finally the forest swallowed up the last of the travelers and the boys returned to the monastery in a gently pensive mood.

"So, the parents have left," said the proctor.

Now they began to look each other over and become acquainted; first, of course, the boys within each room. Inkpots were filled with ink and the lamps with kerosene, books and notebooks were laid out. They all tried to make themselves at home in their new rooms, a process during which they kept eying each other with curiosity, started their first conversations, asked each other where they were from, what school they had attended, and kept reminding each other of the state examination through which they had sweated together. Groups formed around certain desks and entered into extended conversations; here and there a boyish laugh ventured forth, and by evening the roommates were better acquainted than passengers at the end of a long voyage.

Four of Hans' companions in Hellas made an outstanding impression; the rest were more or less above average. First there was Otto Hartner, the son of a Stuttgart professor, a talented, calm, self-assured boy with perfect manners. He was tall, well-proportioned, well-dressed and impressed the room with his firm and decisive manner. Then there was Karl Hamel, the son of a mayor of a small village in the Swabian Alb. It took some time to get to know him for he was full of contradictions and would drop his seemingly phlegmatic attitude only rarely. Yet when he did he would become impassioned, extroverted and violent, but not for long; then he would crawl back into his shell and there was no telling whether he was merely being cagey or a truly dispassionate observer.

A striking though less complicated person was a Hermann Heilner, a Black Forest boy from a good home. It became apparent the first day that he was a poet and esthete and it was rumored that he had written his German exam composition in hexameters. His talk was abundant and vivacious; he owned a good violin and seemed to be exactly what he was on the surface: a youthful combination of sentimentality and lightheadedness. Less obvious was a certain depth of character. He was precocious in body and soul and even now made tentative sallies in directions that were entirely his own.

However, Hellas' most unusual occupant was Emil Lucius, a secretive, wan, flaxen-haired little fellow as tough, industrious and ascetic as an old peasant. Despite his slight and immature build and features, he did not give the impression of being a boy but had something altogether grown-up about him, as though he were completed and nothing could any longer be changed. The very first day, while the others were bored, or gabbed, Lucius sat calm and relaxed over a grammar, his thumbs plugged in his ears, and studied away as if he had lost years to make up for.

This sly and reticent fellow's tricks were not discovered for some time, but then he was unmasked as such a crafty cheapskate and egoist that his perfection in these vices gained him a kind of re-

spect, or at least acceptance by the boys. He had
evolved a cunning system of usury whose fine
points were revealed only by degrees and aroused
genuine astonishment. The first step in this program occurred every morning, when Lucius appeared as either the first or last person in the washroom so as to be able to use someone else's soap or
towel, or both, in order to conserve his own. In
that way he contrived to make his own towel last
from two to three weeks. However, the students
were supposed to change their towels once a
week, and each Monday the head proctor per-
sonally oversaw this transaction. Therefore Lucius
hung a clean towel on his nail on Monday morning only to take it away again at noon, fold it
neatly, replace it in his closet and hang the clean
old towel back on the nail. His soap was an
especially hard brand and it was difficult to use
much of it at any one time. Thus one bar would
last him months. Lucius' appearance, however, suffered no neglect. He always looked well groomed,
his hair neatly combed and parted, and he took
exemplary care of his linen and clothes.

Once the boys were done in the washroom,
they went to breakfast, which consisted of a cup
of coffee, a lump of sugar and a roll. Most of them
did not consider this very rich fare, for young
people tend to have a considerable appetite after
eight hours of sleep. Lucius was perfectly satisfied, saved his daily lump of sugar and always
found takers: two lumps for a penny, or a writing-

pad for twenty-five. It follows that he preferred to work in the light of his roommates' lamps in order to conserve his own supply of expensive kerosene. Not that he was the child of poor parents. On the contrary, they were really quite well off. For as a rule it is the case that the children of impoverished parents don't know how to save and economize, but always need exactly as much as they happen to have and don't know what it means to put something aside.

However, Lucius' system not only extended to the realm of tangible goods and personal ownership; in intellectual matters too he sought to gain an advantage whenever he could. Yet he was clever enough never to forget that intellectual property has only relative value. Therefore he concentrated his efforts on those subjects whose assiduous cultivation might bear fruit in a future examination while he was satisfied with middling grades in the rest of his subjects. Whatever he learned and accomplished he would evaluate only as it compared with the achievements of his fellow students; if he had had the choice, he would have preferred to come in first in class with half as much knowledge than come in second with double the amount. Therefore you could see him working in the evening undisturbed by the noise his roommates made while they played, and the occasional glance he threw in their direction was without envy, even cheerful, for if all the others were as industrious as he, his efforts would not have proved worthwhile.

No one held these tricks and dodges against the sly little grind. But like all who exaggerate and seek excessive profit, it was not long before he made a fool of himself. As all instruction in the academy was free of charge, it occurred to Lucius to take advantage of the situation by taking violin lessons. Not that he had had previous instruction or an ear or aptitude or even enjoyed music! But he decided it would be possible to learn to play the violin the way you could learn to master arithmetic and Latin. He had heard music might be of use to his career and that it made you popular, and in any case, it cost nothing, for the academy even provided a practice violin.

Herr Haas, the music instructor, was ready to throw a fit when Lucius came and asked to take violin lessons. For Haas knew him only too well from the singing class, where Lucius' efforts proved highly amusing to the rest of the students but brought him, the instructor, close to despair. He sought to dissuade Lucius from this project; yet Lucius was not someone easily dissuaded. He put on a delicate and modest smile, invoked his rights and declared his passion for music to be overpowering. Thus Lucius was given the worst practice violin, received two lessons a week, and practiced each day for one half-hour. However, after he had practiced once, his roommates in-

formed him it was the last time, and forthwith
forbade him his merciless scraping in their presence. From that day on Lucius and his violin
moved restlessly about the monastery in search of
quiet nooks to practice, and strange squeaking and
whining noises would emanate to frighten anyone
in the vicinity. Heilner, the poet, said it sounded
as though the tortured old violin were screaming
out of all its wormholes for mercy. Because Lucius
made no progress, the instructor became distraught
and impolite, and as a consequence Lucius practiced even more frantically, his self-satisfied shopkeeper's countenance beginning to show signs of
distress. It was truly tragic: when the teacher
declared him completely incompetent and refused
to continue the lessons, the mad pupil next chose
the piano and spent further agonizing months
until he was worn out and quietly gave up struggling with this instrument. In later years, however,
when the conversation turned to music he quietly
hinted that he himself had learned to play the
violin and the piano at one time but, due to cir-
cumstances beyond his control, had become alienated slowly but surely from these beautiful arts.

Hellas therefore was often in a position to be
amused by its comical occupants, for Heilner, the
esthete, also was the instigator of many ridiculous
scenes. Karl Hamel played the role of the ironical
and witty observer. He was one year older than
the others—which gave him a certain advantage.
Yet he was not really respected. He was moody

and about once a week he felt the need to test his physical prowess in a fight and then he became wild and almost cruel.

Hans Giebenrath watched all these doings with astonishment and went his own quiet way as a good but unexciting companion. He was industrious, almost as industrious as Lucius, and he enjoyed the respect of all his roommates with the exception of Heilner, who had hoisted a banner proclaiming himself a "lighthearted genius" and would occasionally mock Hans for being a grind. These rapidly growing boys got along very well, on the whole, even if the nightly roughhouse in the dormitory led to occasional excesses. For everyone was eager to feel mature and to justify the unaccustomed "Mister" with which the teachers honored them for their good behavior and scholarly seriousness. They all looked back on their grammar-school days with as much disdain as university students on their high-school days. But every so often unadulterated boyishness would break through the dignified façade and assert its rights. At those times the dormitory would resound with the uproar of rushing feet and boyish oaths.

For a teacher at such an institution it ought to be an instructive and delicious experience to observe how such a horde of boys, after it has lived together for several weeks, begins to resemble a chemical mixture in which drifting clouds and flakes compact, dissolve again and re-form until a

HERMANN HESSE

number of firm configurations result. After the
first shyness has been overcome and after they have
all become sufficiently acquainted, there begins
a mingling and searching; groups form and friendships and antipathies become evident. Boys who
had been schoolmates before or who came from
the same region would link up only rarely. Most
boys were on the lookout for new acquaintances—
town boys for farm boys, mountain boys for low-
landers—all in accordance with a secret longing
for variety and completion. The young beings
groped around indecisively for what suited them
best, and out of the awareness of sameness grew
the desire for differentiation, and in some cases
awakened for the first time the growing germ of a
personality out of its childhood slumber. In-
describable little scenes of affection and jealousy
took place, grew into pacts of friendship or into declared and stubborn animosities and ended, as
the case might be, in a tender relationship with
long walks or in wrestling and boxing matches.

Hans did not engage outwardly in any of these
activities. Karl Hamel had made him an explicit
and stormy offer of his friendship—Hans had
shied back, startled. Thereupon Hamel at once
became friends with a boy from Sparta. Hans remained alone. A powerful longing made the land
of friendship glow with alluring colors on the
horizon and drew him quietly in that direction.
Only his shyness held him back. The gift for
entering into an affectionate relationship had with-

ered during his motherless childhood and any demonstration of feelings filled him with horror. Then there was his boyish pride and last but not least his merciless ambition. He was not like Lucius, he was genuinely interested in knowledge, but he resembled Lucius in that he sought to disassociate himself from everything that might keep him from his work.

So he remained anchored to his desk but pined with jealousy when he watched how happy their friendship made the others. Karl Hamel had not been the right one, but if someone else were to approach him and vigorously seek to win his friendship, he would respond gladly. Like a wallflower he stayed in the background waiting for someone to fetch him, someone more courageous and stronger than himself to tear him away and force him into happiness.

Because their schoolwork, especially Hebrew, kept everyone busy, the first weeks passed in a great rush. The many small lakes and ponds that abound in the Maulbronn region reflected the late autumn sky, discolored ash trees, birches and oaks and long twilit evenings. Fall storms romped through beautiful forests cleaning the dried leaves off the branches, and a light hoarfrost had fallen several times.

The poetic Hermann Heilner had vainly sought to find a congenial friend, and now he roamed every day during free hour through the forests by himself, showing a particular liking for a melan-

choly brown pond surrounded by reeds and over-
hung with dried tree crowns. This sad and beautiful forest nook proved immensely attractive to his
lyrical temperament. Here he dreamily traced circles in the water with a sprig, read Lenau's *Reed
Songs*, and reclining on the reeds themselves, contemplated the autumnal theme of dying and the
transience of all living matter while the falling
leaves and the wind sighing through the stark
trees added gloomy chords. Frequently he pulled
out his small black notebook to write a verse or
two.

He was doing precisely that one overcast afternoon in late October when Hans Giebenrath, also
by himself, happened on the same locale. He saw
the fledgling poet sitting on the narrow boardwalk
of the small sluice gate, notebook in lap, a sharpened pencil stuck pensively in his mouth. An open
book lay by his side. Slowly Hans stepped closer.

"Hello, Heilner. What are you doing there?"

"Reading Homer. And you, Giebenrath, my
boy?"

"Do you think I don't know what you're up to?"

"Well?"

"You're writing a poem, of course."

"You think so?"

"Certainly."

"Have a seat."

Giebenrath sat down next to Heilner on the
board, let his legs dangle over the water, and
watched one brown leaf and then another spiral

down through the cool stillness and settle inaudibly on the water's brownish mirror.

"I must say it's sad here," Hans blurted out.

"Yes, yes."

Both of them had lain down on their backs. They saw little else of their autumnal surroundings but a few slanting treetops and the light blue sky with its drifting cloud islands.

"What beautiful clouds!" Hans said, gazing on high.

"Yes, Giebenrath," Heilner sighed. "If only we could be clouds like that."

"What then?"

"Then we would sail along up there, over woods, villages, entire provinces and countries like beautiful ships. Haven't you ever seen a ship?"

"No, Heilner, have you?"

"Oh yes. My God, you don't understand any of this if all you can do is study and be a drudge."

"So you think I'm a grind?"

"I didn't say that."

"I'm not as silly as you think by a long shot. But go ahead, tell me about your ships."

Heilner turned around on his stomach, almost falling in the water in the process. Now he looked at Hans, his hands propping up his chin.

"I saw ships like that," he went on, "on the Rhine during vacation. One Sunday there was music on the ship, at night, and colored lanterns. The lights were reflected in the water and we sailed downstream with the music. Everyone was drinking Rhine wine and the girls wore white dresses."

Hans listened without replying but he had closed his eyes and saw the ship sail through the night with music and red lights and girls in white dresses.

Heilner went on: "Yes, things were certainly different then. Who knows anything about things like that around here? All these bores and cowards who grind away and work their fingers to the bone and don't realize that there's something higher than the Hebrew alphabet. You're no different."

Hans kept silent. This Heilner fellow certainly was a strange one. A romantic, a poet. As everyone knew, he worked hardly at all and still he knew quite a bit, he knew how to give good answers, and at the same time despised his learning.

"We're reading Homer," he went on in the same mocking tone, "as though the *Odyssey* were a cookbook. Two verses an hour and then the whole thing is masticated word by word and inspected until you're ready to throw up. But at the end of the hour the professor will say: 'Notice how nicely the poet has turned this phrase! This has afforded you an insight into the secret of poetic creativity!' Just like a little icing around the aorists and particles so you won't choke on them completely. I don't have any use for that kind of Homer. Anyway, what does all this old Greek stuff matter to us? If one of us ever tried to live a little like a Greek, he'd be out on his tail. And our room is called 'Hellas'! Pure mockery! Why isn't it called 'wastepaper basket' or 'monkey cage' or 'sweatshop'? All this classical stuff is a big fake."

He spat into the air.

"Were you working on a poem before?" Hans now asked.

"Yes."

"About what?"

"Here, about the pond and fall."

"Can I see it?"

"No, it's not finished."

"But when it's finished?"

"Sure, if you want to."

The two got up and slowly walked back to the monastery.

"There, have you actually noticed how beautiful that is?" Heilner said as they passed the Paradise. "Halls, bow windows, cloisters, refectories, gothic and romanesque, all of it rich with artistry and made with an artist's hand. And who is all this magic for? For a few dozen boys who are poor and are supposed to become pastors. The state seems to be swimming in it."

Hans thought about nothing but Heilner for the rest of the afternoon. What an odd fellow! Hans' worries and desires simply did not exist for him. He had thoughts and words of his own, he lived a richer and freer life, suffered strange ailments and seemed to despise everything around him. He understood the beauty of the ancient columns and walls. And he practiced the mysterious and unusual art of mirroring his soul in verse and of constructing a semblance of life for himself out of his imagination. He was quick and untamable and had more fun in a day than Hans in an entire year. He was melancholy and seemed to relish his own sadness like an unusual condition, alien and delicious.

That very evening Heilner treated the entire room to a performance of his checkered and striking personality. One of their companions, a showoff and mean-spirited fellow by the name of Otto Wenger, picked a quarrel with him. For a short while Heilner stayed calm, witty and superior, then he let his impulse carry him away and he gave Wenger a slap in the face. At once the two became passionately and inextricably entangled, drifted and tumbled like a rudderless ship in fits and jerks and half-circles through Hellas, along walls, over chairs, across the floor, neither saying a word, gasping, fuming and foaming at the mouth. The roommates watched this with critical expressions, avoiding the tangle of arms and legs, salvaging their legs, desks and lamps, awaiting the outcome eagerly and with high expectations. After several minutes Heilner rose, not without some effort, freed himself and just stood there breathing heavily. He looked mutilated, his eyes were red, his collar torn and he had a hole in his pants knee. His opponent was about to renew his onslaught but Heilner just crossed his arms and said haughtily: "I won't go on—if you want, go ahead, hit me." Otto Wenger left cursing. Heilner leaned against his desk, fiddled with his lamp, plunged his hands in his pants pockets and seemed to fall into a reflective far-off mood. Suddenly tears broke from his eyes, one after the other, more and more. This was unheard of. For crying was beyond doubt considered the most despicable thing an academy student could do. And Heilner did nothing to try to conceal it. He did not leave the room, he simply stood there, his face pale from the exertion, looking at the lamp; he did not wipe his tears, did not even take his hands out of his pockets. The others stood around him, curiosity and malice in their faces until Hartner planted himself in front of him and said: "Hey, Heilner, aren't you ashamed of yourself?"

The tearful Heilner slowly looked around, like someone who has just awakened from a deep sleep.

"Feel ashamed—in front of you?" Then he said loud and derisively: "No, my friend."

He wiped his face, smiled angrily, blew out his lamp and left the room.

Hans Giebenrath had not moved from his desk during the entire incident and only glanced in astonishment at Heilner. Fifteen minutes later, he dared to go look for him. He saw him sitting in the dark chilly dormitory hall in one of the deep window embrasures, immobile, gazing out into the cloister. From the back his shoulders and his narrow, sharply chiseled head looked unusually serious and unboyish. He did not move as Hans stepped up to him. After a while he asked hoarsely, without facing Hans: "What's up?"

"It's me," said Hans timidly.

"What do you want?"

"Nothing."

"Well, in that case, why don't you leave?"

Hans was hurt and was about to do just that. Heilner held him back.

"Don't go," he said with a lightness that did not sound convincing. "I didn't mean it like that."

Now they faced each other and at this moment each took his first serious look at the other and tried to imagine that these boyishly smooth features concealed a particular personality and a soul of its very own.

Hermann Heilner slowly extended his arm, took Hans by the shoulder and drew him to him until their faces almost touched. Then Hans was startled to feel the other's lips touch his.

His heart was seized by an unaccustomed tremor. This being together in the dark dormitory and this sudden kiss was something frightening, something new, perhaps something dangerous; it occurred to him how dreadful it would be if he were caught, for he realized how much more ridiculous and shameful kissing would seem to the others than crying. There was nothing he could say, but the blood rose to his head and he wanted to run away.

An adult witnessing this little scene might have derived a quiet joy from it, from the tenderly inept shyness and the earnestness of these two narrow faces, both of them handsome, promising, boyish yet marked half with childish grace and half with shy yet attractive adolescent defiance.

The young students had now grown accustomed to one another. They each had formed some picture of the others and numerous friendships had been struck. There were couples who learned Hebrew verbs together or painted, went for walks or read Schiller. There were students who were bad in math but good in Latin who had paired up with students good in math but bad in Latin so as to enjoy the fruits of cooperation. But there were also friendships whose basis was a kind of contract and sharing of tangible goods. Thus the much-envied owner of the whole ham had found his better half in the person of a gardener's son from Stammheim whose closet floor was piled high with apples. Once while eating his ham he asked the gardener's son for an apple, offering him a slice of ham in exchange. They promptly sat down together, and their careful conversation revealed that there were many more hams where this came from and the apple owner too could draw freely on his father's supply. In that fashion a solid friendship came into being, one which outlasted many a more idealistic and impetuous pact.

There were only a few boys who remained single, and among them was Lucius, whose acquisitive devotion to the art of music was still in full bloom at that time.

There also were some badly matched pairs. Hermann Heilner and Hans Giebenrath, the light-headed and the conscientious, the poet and the grind, were regarded as possibly the most ill-matched. Although both were considered to be two of the brightest and most gifted students, Heilner enjoyed the half-mocking reputation of being a genius while Hans bore the stigma of being a model boy. Still, since everyone else was preoccupied with his own friendship, these two were left pretty much to themselves.

Despite these personal interests and experiences, their schoolwork did not receive short shrift. On the contrary, school was rather the main part alongside which Lucius' music, Heilner's poetry and all pacts, transactions and occasional fights played a minor and diversionary role. Especially Hebrew kept all of them on their toes. The peculiar ancient language of Jehovah, an uncouth, withered and yet secretly living tree, took on an alien, gnarled and puzzling form before the boys' eyes, catching their attention through unusual linkages and astonishing them with remarkably colored and fragrant blossoms. In its branches, hollows and roots lived friendly or gruesome thousand-year-old ghosts: phantastically fearsome dragons, lovely naïve girls and wrinkled sages next to handsome boys and calm-eyed girls or quarrelsome women. What had sounded remote and dreamlike in the Lutheran Bible was now lent blood in its true and coarse character, as well as a voice and an old, cumbersome but tenacious and ominous life. That at least was the way it appeared to Heilner, who cursed the entire Pentateuch on the hour and still found more life and spirit in it than many a patient drudge who knew the entire vocabulary and pronounced everything correctly.

In addition there was the New Testament where everything was more delicate, bright and intimate and whose language, though less ancient and profound and rich, was filled with an eager and imaginative young spirit.

And there was the *Odyssey* whose vigorously sonorous, measured numbers gave an intimation of a vanished, clearly articulated and joyous life. Next to this the historians Xenophon and Livy disappeared or rather stood, as lesser luminaries, to the side, modest and almost pale in comparison.

With some astonishment Hans discovered how different all things looked to his friend than to him. Nothing was abstract for Heilner, nothing he could not have imagined and colored with his fantasy. When this was impossible he turned away, bored. Mathematics, as far as he was concerned, was a Sphinx charged with deceitful puzzles whose cold malicious gaze transfixed her victims, and he gave the monster a wide berth.

The friendship between the two was an unusual one. For Heilner it was a delightful luxury, a convenience or merely a quirk, whereas Hans cherished it like a proudly guarded treasure, but a treasure that could become a burden. Until recently Hans had always done his homework in the evening. Now Hermann, tired of studying, would come over to his desk, pull away his books and demand his attention. It got so bad that Hans, much as he liked his friend, actually trembled at his coming and would work hurriedly and with redoubled effort during the regularly scheduled study hours. The situation became even more difficult when Heilner began to oppose his industry with theoretical arguments.

"That's hackwork," he would announce. "You're not doing any of this work voluntarily but only because you're afraid of the teachers or of your old man. What do you get from being first or second in class? I'm twentieth, and just as smart as any of you grinds."

Hans was equally horrified to discover how Heilner treated his books. One day Hans had left his atlas in the lecture hall and since he wanted to prepare himself for an upcoming geography lesson he borrowed Heilner's. With disgust he noted that entire pages had been dirtied with pencil markings. The west coast of the Iberian peninsula had been reshaped to form a grotesque profile with a nose reaching from Porto to Lisbon, the area around Cape Finisterre stylized into a curly coiffure while Cape St. Vincent formed the nicely twirled point of a beard. It was the same from page to page; the white backs of the maps were covered with caricatures and epigrams, nor was there a lack of ink spots. Hans was in the habit of treating his books like sacred objects, like jewels, and he considered such derring-do as both a sacrilege and a heroic if criminal deed.

At times it seemed as if Hans were merely a convenient plaything for his friend—let's say a kind of housecat—and Hans himself felt that occasionally. Yet Heilner was truly attached to him because he needed him. He had to have someone who would listen quietly and eagerly when he delivered his revolutionary speeches about school and life in general. And he also needed someone to console him, someone in whose lap he could rest his head when he was depressed. Like all such people, the young poet suffered from attacks of irrational and slightly coquettish melancholy whose causes were many, having to do with the painful transition from childhood to adolescence, with an excess of premonitions, energy and desires which, however, did not lack a goal, and also with the incomprehensible dark drives of early manhood. He had a pathological need to be pitied and fondled. Before he had come to school he had been his mother's pet and now, as long as he was not ready for womanly love, his accommodating friend had to fulfill the role of comforter.

In the evening he often came deeply depressed to Hans, abducted him from his work and asked him to go with him to the dormitory. There, in the cold hall or in the spacious, darkening oratory they walked up and down or sat shivering in an alcove. Heilner then would hold forth with any number of plaintive grievances in the manner of romantic youths who have read Heine and become enraptured with a somewhat childish sorrow. This impressed Hans, though he could not quite understand it, and even infected him on occasions. The sensitive *bel esprit* was particularly vulnerable to these attacks during inclement weather; his moaning and groaning would reach its apogee usually on evenings when the rain clouds of a late fall evening darkened the sky, with the moon slinking through gloomy rifts. Then he would luxuriate in Ossianic moods and dissolve in melancholy which poured over the innocent Hans in the form of sighs, speeches and verse.

Oppressed and pained by these agonizing scenes, Hans would plunge into his work during the remaining hours, work which became more and more difficult for him. The return of his old headaches did not surprise him particularly; but that he experienced more and more inactive, listless hours and had to force himself to do the most rudimentary things worried him deeply.

He sensed how this friendship exhausted him, how a part of him which had been hale became sick. But the gloomier and more tearful Heilner became, the more Hans pitied him and the tenderer and prouder grew his awareness of being indispensable to his friend.

Of course he also realized that this sickly melancholy was only the ejection of superfluous and unhealthy energies and not really an integral part of Heilner, whom he admired faithfully and genuinely. When his friend recited his poetry or talked about his poetic ideals or delivered impassioned monologues from Schiller or Shakespeare—all the while gesturing dramatically—Hans felt as though Heilner, due to a magic gift he himself lacked, was walking on air, moved about with supernal freedom to disappear from him and the likes of him on winged sandals like a Homeric messenger. The world of the poets had been of little importance to Hans, but now for the first time he let the force of beautiful rhetoric, deceptive images and caressing rhymes flow over him, and his admiration for this new world fused into a single feeling of veneration for his friend.

Meanwhile dark stormy November days came during which you could work at your desk for only a few hours without lamplight, and black nights during which the storm would drive huge tumbling clouds through dark heights and the wind groaned and quarreled around the ancient monastery building. The trees now had lost all their leaves—with the exception of the gnarled oaks, the royalty of a countryside rich in trees, which still rustled their dead leaves louder and more grumpily than all other trees combined. Heilner was in a sour mood and recently he had preferred not to sit with Hans but to give vent to his feelings on his violin in a remote practice room or to pick fights with his companions.

One evening as he entered the room, he found

Lucius practicing before the music stand. Angrily he left. When he returned half an hour later Lucius was still going strong.

"You know it's about time for you to quit," fumed Heilner. "Other people would like to have a chance to practice too. Your ungodly noises are a curse anyway."

Lucius would not budge. Heilner began to lose his temper, and when Lucius resumed his scraping, he kicked over the music stand, the sheet music scattering on the floor, the top of the music stand slamming into Lucius' face. Lucius bent down for the music.

"I'll report you to the headmaster," he said decisively.

"Fine," screamed Heilner, "and you can tell him too that I gave you a kick in the ass." And he was about to step into action.

Lucius fled to the side and made it to the door, his antagonist in hot pursuit, and there ensued a noisy chase through the corridors, halls, across stairways to the remotest part of the monastery where the headmaster resided in calm and dignity. Heilner caught up with the fugitive in front of the headmaster's study just as Lucius had knocked and stood in the open door, so Lucius received the promised kick at the last possible moment and shot like a bomb into the holy of holies.

This was an unheard-of incident. The very next morning the headmaster delivered a brilliant lecture on the subject of the degeneration of youth.

Lucius listened with a thoughtful and appreciative expression while Heilner was sentenced to a long period of room arrest.

"Such punishment as this," the headmaster thundered at him, "has not been meted out for years and years. I am going to make very sure that you will remember it for the next ten. You others should regard Heilner as a frightful example."

The entire school glanced shyly at Heilner, who stood there pale and stubborn and looked unblinking directly into the headmaster's eyes. Many admired him in secret. Yet at the end of the lecture, as everyone was noisily filing out, Heilner was left by himself and avoided like a leper. It took courage to stand by him now.

Hans Giebenrath did not stand by him either. It was his duty—he certainly realized this and suffered from his awareness of his cowardly behavior. Unhappy and ashamed, he hid in an alcove not daring to raise his eyes. He felt the urge to go to his friend and he would have given much if he could have done so without anyone noticing. But someone who has been given as serious a sentence as Heilner might as well be blackballed for the time it takes people to speak to you again. Everyone knows that the culprit will be watched and that it is risky and gives you a bad reputation if you have anything to do with him. The benefits the state bestows on its charges have to have a corresponding measure of sharp and strict discipline. The headmaster had said as much in his first address. Hans was aware of this. And in the struggle between duty to his friend and his ambition, his loyalty succumbed. It was his ambition to succeed, to pass his examination with the highest honors, and to play a role in life, but not a romantic or dangerous one. Thus he remained in his corner hideout. There was still time to do the courageous thing, but from moment to moment this became increasingly difficult, and before he had given it any real thought, his inaction had turned into betrayal.

Heilner did not fail to notice it. The passionate boy felt how he was being avoided and he understood why, but he had counted on Hans. Compared to the woe and outrage he now felt his former melancholy seemed barren and silly. For just a moment he stopped beside Giebenrath. He looked pale and haughty and softly he said:

"You're nothing but a coward, Giebenrath—go to hell." And then he left, whistling softly, his hands stuck in his pants pockets.

Fortunately the boys were kept busy by other thoughts and activities. A few days after this incident it suddenly began to snow. Then there was a stretch of clear frosty weather. You could enjoy snowball fights, go ice-skating. Now all of them suddenly realized and discussed the fact that Christmas and their first vacation were imminent. The boys began to pay less attention to Heilner, who went about the school with his head held high, a haughty expression, talking to no one and

frequently penning verses in his notebook, a notebook wrapped in black oilcloth which bore the
inscription "Songs of a Monk."

Hoarfrost and frozen snow clung to the oaks,
alders, beeches and willows in configurations of
fantastic delicacy. On the ponds the crystal-clear
ice crackled in the frost. The cloister yard looked
like a sculpture garden. A festive mood spread
through the rooms and the joy of anticipating
Christmas even lent the two imperturbably correct
professors a weak aura of benevolence. No one
among the students and teachers remained indiffer-
ent to Christmas. Heilner began to look somewhat less grim and miserable, and Lucius tried to
decide which books and what pair of shoes to take
home with him. The letters the parents sent contained promising intimations: inquiries about favorite wishes, reports of "Bake Day," hints about
forthcoming surprises and expressions of gladness
about the imminent reunion.

Just before the beginning of the vacation the
entire school—particularly Hellas—witnessed another amusing incident. The students had decided
to invite the teachers to a Christmas soirée in Hellas, the largest of the rooms. One oration, two reci-
tations, a flute solo and a violin duet had been
planned. But more than anything else the boys
wanted to include a humorous number in their
programs. They discussed and negotiated, made and
dropped suggestions without being able to agree.
Then Karl Hamel casually remarked that the most

amusing number might be a violin solo by Lucius. That hit the spot. A combination of promises, threats and imprecations forced the unhappy musician to lend his services. The program, which the teachers received with a polite invitation, listed as a feature attraction: "*Silent Night*, air for violin, performed by Emile Lucius, chamber virtuoso." The latter appellation was Lucius' reward for his zealous endeavors in the remote music room.

Headmaster, professors, tutors, music teacher and the dean of boys were invited and all came to attend the festivities. The music teacher's forehead broke out in cold sweat when Lucius, groomed and combed and sporting a black suit he had borrowed from Hartner, stepped up to the music stand with a gently smiling modesty. Just the way he clenched his bow was an invitation to laughter, and *Silent Night*, under his fingers, turned into a gripping lament, a groaning, painful song of suffering. He had to start over twice, ripped and hacked the melody apart, kept the beat with his foot and labored like a lumberjack in winter.

The headmaster nodded cheerfully in the direction of the music teacher, who was ashen with outrage.

When Lucius launched into the third start and got stuck this time too, he lowered his violin, turned to the audience and excused himself: "It just won't go. But I only started to play the violin this fall."

"It's all right, Lucius," said the headmaster, "we

are grateful to you for your efforts. Just keep at it. *Per aspera ad astra.*"

Early in the morning of the twenty-fourth of December, the dormitories resounded with noise and activity. A thick layer of finely leafed ice-flowers blossomed on the windowpanes. The water in the washbasin was frozen and a keen wind cut across the cloister yard, but this did not bother anyone. In the dining hall large tureens steamed with coffee, and soon afterward the boys, insulated in thick coats and shawls, wandered in dark clumps across the white fields and through the hushed forest toward the remote railroad station. They were all chattering, joking and laughing loudly, and yet each boy's unexpressed thoughts turned to secret wishes, joys and expectations. Throughout the entire land—in towns, villages and isolated farmhouses—they knew that parents and brothers and sisters were expecting them in warm, festively decorated rooms. For most of them this was their first experience of taking a trip home for Christmas and most of them were aware of being awaited with love and pride.

They waited on the bitterly cold platform of the little railroad station in the middle of the forest and at no time had they been as united, tolerant and cheerful as now. Only Heilner remained by himself and silent, and when the train pulled into the station he waited until his fellow students had mounted before he found a compartment where he could be alone. Hans saw him once more as they changed trains at the next station, but his feeling of shame and regret vanished beneath the excitement and joy of the trip home.

There he was met by a satisfied delighted father and a table richly decked with gifts. However, the Giebenrath household could not produce a genuine Christmas atmosphere. There were no Christmas songs, no spontaneous joy in the festivities; there was no mother and no Christmas tree. Giebenrath senior lacked the art of celebrating a feast. But he was proud of his boy and he had not been stingy with presents. And Hans was used to the situation and did not feel that anything was lacking.

People felt that he did not look well, or well fed, and was far too pale and they doubted whether he got enough to eat at the monastery. He denied this emphatically and assured everyone that he was in good shape except for his frequent headaches. The pastor assured him in this matter by telling him that he had suffered the same headaches while he was young, and thus all problems were solved.

The river was frozen clear across, and during the holidays it was covered with ice-skaters from morning till night. Hans spent almost every day entirely out of doors wearing a new suit and the green academy cap. He had outgrown his former schoolmates and lived in a much-envied higher realm.

Chapter Four

I T IS COMMON knowledge that one or more
students will drop out during the course of
their four years at the academy. Occasionally one
of them will die and be buried while the other
students sing hymns, or be taken home with a
cortege of friends. At other times a boy will run
away or be expelled because of some outrageous
misdemeanor. Occasionally—though rarely, and
then only in the senior classes—it happens that a
boy in despair will find an escape from his adolescent agonies by drowning or shooting himself.

Hans' class, too, was to lose several of its members, and by a strange coincidence it happened
that all of them had roomed in Hellas.

One of the occupants of Hellas was a modest,
flaxen-haired little fellow named Hindinger, whom
they called Hindu. He was the son of a tailor from
predominantly Catholic Allgäu, and was so quiet
that only his departure made people take notice of
him, and even then not for long. As the desk-
neighbor of the parsimonious Lucius, Hindu had
had, in his own friendly and unassuming way, a
little more to do with him than with the others,

but he had had no real friends. Not until they actually missed him did his roommates realize that they were fond of him as a good neighbor who had been undemanding and had represented a calm point in the often excited life of Hellas.

One day in January he joined the ice-skaters who were going out to cavort on the Horsepond. He himself did not own a pair of skates and simply wanted to watch the others. Soon he began to feel the cold and stomped around the edge of the pond trying to keep warm. While doing so he began to run, lost his way, and came upon another little lake which, because of its warmer and stronger springs, had only a thin sheet of ice. As he stepped across it to go through the reeds, the ice broke, small and light though he was. Close to the edge, he struggled and screamed desperately and then sank unseen into the dark coolness.

No one noticed he was missing until the first lesson at two o'clock.

"Where's Hindinger?" the tutor called out.

No one answered.

"Someone go look for him in Hellas."

But he was not to be found there either.

"He must be delayed somewhere. Let's begin the lesson without him. We are on page forty-seven, verse seven. But I insist that there be no repetition of this sort of thing. You must be punctual."

When the clock struck three and there still was no sign of Hindinger, the tutor became nervous.

He sent for the headmaster, who immediately came to the lecture hall and went through a long series of questions. He then dispatched ten students, a proctor and a tutor to search for Hindinger. Those who stayed behind were assigned a written exercise.

Around four o'clock the tutor entered the hall without knocking and began whispering in the headmaster's ear.

"Quiet, everyone," demanded the headmaster. The students sat stock-still in their benches and looked expectantly at him.

"Your friend Hindinger," he went on more softly, "it appears has drowned in one of the ponds. Now you must go help find him. Professor Meyer will lead the way. Your orders are to follow and obey him and to do nothing on your own initiative."

Shocked, whispering among themselves, they got underway with the professor in the lead. A couple of men from town with ropes, boards and wooden poles joined the hurried procession. It was bitter cold and the sun was just about to slip behind the woods.

Just as the small stiff body was recovered and placed on a stretcher in the snow-covered reeds, it became dusk. The students stood in disarray like frightened birds, staring at the corpse and rubbing their stiff, discolored fingers. Not until their drowned comrade was being carried before them on his stretcher were their numb hearts suddenly touched by dread. They smelled death as a deer smells hunters.

Hans Giebenrath found himself walking next to his former friend, the poet Heilner, in that pitiful and freezing little group. They became aware of each other's proximity when they both stumbled over the same unevenness in the field. Perhaps it was the sight of death that overwhelmed and convinced them momentarily of the futility of all selfishness. In any case, when Hans saw his friend's pale face so near, he suddenly felt a deep, inexplicable ache and reached impulsively for his hand. But Heilner drew back at once and cast an offended and angry look to the side. Then he dropped back to the very rear of the procession.

At that point the other boy's heart trembled with woe and shame. As he stumbled on across the frozen wastes, there was nothing Hans could do to keep his tears from trickling down his ice-cold cheeks. He realized that there are certain sins and omissions beyond forgiveness and repentance and it seemed to him that the stretcher bore not the tailor's little son but Heilner, who now took all the pain and anger caused by Hans' faithlessness with him far into another world where people were judged not by their grades and examination marks and scholastic success but solely in accord with the purity or impurity of their consciences.

When they reached the road, they proceeded swiftly to the main monastery, where the entire staff with the headmaster in the lead stood at attention for the dead Hindinger who, if he had been alive, would have quailed at the mere thought of such an honor. The teachers apparently regarded a dead student very differently from a living one. They realized for a fleeting moment how irrecoverable and unique is each life and youth, on whom they perpetrated so much thoughtless harm at other times.

During the evening and all next day, the presence of the unassuming corpse continued to exert its spell. It softened, muted and wreathed all activity and talk, so that for a brief time quarrels, anger, noise and laughter were invisible, like wood-nymphs who disappear briefly from a lake, leaving it tranquil and seemingly unpopulated. When two boys discussed their drowned comrade, they now used his full name, for Hindu seemed too undignified for a dead person. The quiet Hindu, who had always been lost in the crowd, now permeated the huge monastery with his name and the fact of his death.

The second day after his death his father came, stayed a few hours in the room where his son lay, was invited to tea by the headmaster, and spent the night in the Stag, a nearby inn.

Then came the burial. The coffin was given a place of honor in the dormitory and the tailor from Allgäu stood beside it, watching everything that was being done. He was a tailor from head to toe; skinny and angular, he wore a black dresscoat with a greenish sheen to it, and narrow, skimpy trousers. In his hand he held a shabby top hat. His small thin face looked grieved, sad and weak, like a penny-candle in the wind; he was both embarrassed and overawed by the headmaster and the professors.

At the last moment, just before the pallbearers picked up the coffin, the sorry little man stepped forward once more and touched the coffin lid with timid tenderness. He remained there, helplessly fighting his tears, standing in the large quiet room like a withered tree in the winter—it was sorrowful to behold how lost and hopeless and at the mercy of the elements he looked. The pastor took him by the hand and stayed at his side. The tailor put on his fantastically curved top hat and was the first to follow the coffin down the steps, across the cloister, through the old gate and across the white countryside toward the low churchyard wall. While singing hymns at the graveside the students annoyed the music-teacher by not watching his hand beating time. Instead they looked at the lonely, wind-blown figure of the little tailor who stood sad and freezing in the snow, listening with bowed head to the pastor's and headmaster's speeches, nodding to the students, and occasionally fishing with his left hand for a handkerchief in his coat without ever extracting it.

"I could not help imagining my own father standing there like that," Otto Hartner said afterward. Then they all joined in: "Yes, I thought the same thing."

Later on the headmaster brought Hindinger's father to Hellas. "Was one of you particularly close to the deceased?" the headmaster asked. At first no one volunteered and Hindu's father stared with misery and fear at the young faces. Then Lucius stepped forward and Hindinger took his hand, held it a while but did not know what to say and soon left again with a humble nod of the head. Thereupon he took leave of the monastery altogether. He had to travel a whole long day through the bright winter landscape before he reached his home where he could tell his wife in what sort of place their Karl lay buried.

The spell that death had cast over the monastery was soon broken. The teachers were giving reprimands again, the doors were again being slammed and little thought if any was devoted to the former occupant of Hellas. Several boys had contracted colds while standing around that melancholy pond and lay in the infirmary or ran about in felt slippers with shawls wrapped around their throats. Hans Giebenrath had withstood the ordeal intact in health, but he looked older and more serious since the day of misfortune. Something inside him had changed. The boy had become an adolescent, and his soul seemed to have been transferred to another country, where it fluttered about anxiously, knowing no rest. This change was due not so much to shock or sorrow over Hindu's death but to his having suddenly become aware of what he had done to Heilner.

Heilner lay with two other boys in the infirmary. He had to swallow hot tea, and there was ample time to arrange his impressions of Hindinger's death for possible future use in his poetry. Still, he did not seem overly intent on writing poetry at the moment, for he was languishing and said hardly a word to his fellow patients. His isolation, a consequence of his prolonged roomarrest, had wounded and embittered his sensitive spirit. He could not go long without communicating his feelings and thoughts. The teachers kept a sharp eye on him as a dissatisfied troublemaker; the students avoided him; the tutors treated him with mocking goodwill, and his friends Shakespeare, Lenau and Schiller showed him a different, mightier and more spectacular world than his present oppressive and humiliating surroundings. His *Monk Songs*, which at first had struck only a melancholy note of isolation, gradually turned into a collection of bitter and hate-filled verses about the monastery, his teachers and fellow students. He took sour pleasure in his martyrdom, derived satisfaction from being misunderstood, and felt like a young Juvenal with his ruthlessly irreverent monk's verses.

Eight days after the burial, when the two others had recuperated and Heilner was alone in the infirmary, Hans paid him a visit. His greeting sounded timid as he pulled a chair to the bedside and reached for Heilner's hand. Heilner turned morosely toward the wall and seemed quite unapproachable. But Hans refused to be put off. He held on to the hand he had grasped and forced his former friend to look at him. Heilner looked at him with a sneer.

"What are you after anyway?"

Hans did not let his hand go.

"You've got to listen to me," he said. "I was a coward at that time and I let you down. But you know what I'm like: I had made up my mind to stay at the top of the class and if possible to graduate at the head of it. You call me a grind; all right, perhaps that's true. But that was my kind of ideal. I just didn't know any better."

Heilner closed his eyes, and Hans continued in a very soft voice: "You see, I am sorry. I don't know whether you want to become my friend again but you have to forgive me."

Heilner said nothing and did not open his eyes. Everything that was good and glad in him wanted to greet his friend with happy laughter; but he had become so used to playing a harsh and lonely role that he kept the appropriate mask on his face a while longer. Hans persisted.

"You absolutely have to, Heilner! I'd rather end up at the bottom of the class than have things go on like this. If you want, we can become friends again and show the others that we don't need them."

At that point Heilner returned the pressure of Hans' hand and opened his eyes.

After a few days, he too left the infirmary. The newly fashioned friendship caused considerable excitement in the monastery. The two friends were to experience some very unusual weeks together, weeks during which they did not actually have any significant experiences but were filled with a strangely happy feeling of belonging together and being of one mind. This was different from their old friendship. The long separation had changed both of them. Hans had become gentler, warmer, more enthusiastic; Heilner had grown more vigorous and masculine, and both had missed each other so much that their reunion seemed to them like a great experience and a delicious gift.

Both of these precocious boys shyly, though unconsciously, tasted in their friendship the intimation of the delicate secrets of a first love affair. In addition, their pact had the harsh charm of their growing masculinity and the equally harsh spice of defying the entire student body, whose numerous friendships were still harmless games. The students disliked Heilner and could not understand Hans.

The more intimate and happier Hans became with his friend, the more alienated he became from school. The new sensation of happiness rushed through his blood and thoughts like young wine, and Livy and Homer lost all importance and attraction by comparison. The teachers watched in horror as their model student turned into a problem child and succumbed to the bad influence of the dubious Heilner. Teachers dread nothing so much as unusual characteristics in precocious boys during the initial stages of their adolescence. A certain streak of genius makes an ominous impression on them, for there exists a deep gulf between genius and the teaching profession. Anyone with a touch of genius seems to his teachers a freak from the very first. As far as teachers are concerned, they define young geniuses as those who are bad, disrespectful, smoke at fourteen, fall in love at fifteen, can be found at sixteen hanging out in bars, read forbidden books, write scandalous essays, occasionally stare down a teacher in class, are marked in the attendance book as rebels, and are budding candidates for room-arrest. A schoolmaster will prefer to have a couple of dumbheads in his class than a single genius, and if you regard it objectively, he is of course right. His task is not to produce extravagant intellects but good Latinists, arithmeticians and sober decent folk. The question of who suffers more acutely at the other's hands—the teacher at the boy's, or vice versa—who is more of a tyrant, more of a tormentor, and who profanes parts of the other's soul, student or teacher, is something you cannot examine without remembering your own youth in anger and shame. Yet that is not what concerns us here. We have the consolation that among true geniuses the wounds almost always heal. As their personalities develop, they create their art in spite of school. Once dead, and enveloped by the comfortable nimbus of remoteness, they are paraded by the schoolmasters before other generations of students as showpieces and noble examples. Thus the struggle between rule and spirit repeats itself year after year from school to school. The authorities go to infinite pains to nip the few profound or more valuable intellects in the bud. And time and again the ones who are detested by their teachers and frequently punished, the runaways and those expelled, are the ones who afterwards add to society's treasure. But some—and who knows how many? —waste away with quiet obstinacy and finally go under.

According to the good old school precept, as soon as these two strange young boys, Hans and Heilner, came under suspicion, they were treated with redoubled harshness. Only the headmaster, who was proud of Hans as his most zealous student of Hebrew, made an awkward attempt to save him. He invited Hans to his study, the handsome and picturesque belvedere that had been the prior's quarters where, legend has it, Doctor Faustus, who came from the nearby town of Knittlingen, long ago enjoyed his share of Elffinger wine. The headmaster was not a one-sided man, he did not lack insight and practical wisdom, and even possessed a certain measure of goodwill toward his charges whom he liked to call by their first names. His chief failing was a strong streak of vanity, which often let him give in to the temptation of performing little bravura acts on the lectern and did not permit him to suffer to see his own power and authority questioned. He could brook no interference, admit no mistakes. Thus boys who had no wills of their own, and those who were dishonest, got along famously with him. For the same reason, the strong-minded and honest ones had a very hard time of it because the merest hint of disagreement irritated him. He was a virtuoso in the role of fatherly friend with an encouraging look and a deeply moving tone of voice, and it was this role he was playing now.

"Have a seat, Giebenrath," he said in a man-to-man tone, once he had given a vigorous handshake to the boy who had entered so timidly. "I'd like to have a word with you. But I can call you Hans, can't I?"

"Please do, sir."

"You have probably noticed yourself that your work has not been quite up to par in the last few weeks—at least in Hebrew. Until a short while ago you probably were our best Hebraist, that's why it hurts me to notice such a sudden slackening off. Perhaps Hebrew doesn't give you as much pleasure as it used to?"

"Oh no, but it does, sir."

"Think about it a little! Things like that do happen. Perhaps your interest has switched to another subject?"

"No it hasn't, sir."

"Really not? Well, then we have to look for a cause elsewhere. Couldn't you help me find it?"

"I don't know. . . . I've always done my assignments. . . ."

"Of course, my boy, of course. But *differendum est inter et inter*. Naturally you've done your assignments, you didn't have much choice, did you? But you used to accomplish a great deal more than that. You worked harder, or at least you were more interested. And I am asking myself why has your industry lapsed all of a sudden? You aren't sick, are you?"

"No."

"Or do you have headaches? You don't look as well as you sometimes do."

"Yes, I have headaches every so often."

"Is the daily work load too much for you?"

"Oh no, by no means."

"Or are you doing outside reading? Be honest."

"No, sir. I read hardly anything on the side."

"But then I don't quite understand, my dear boy. Something must be wrong somewhere. Will you promise me to make a little more of an effort?"

Hans placed his hand in the outstretched right of the mighty man who regarded him with a benign and serious look.

"That's the way, that's the way, my boy. Just don't let up or you'll get dragged beneath the wheel."

As he pressed Hans' hand, the relieved boy headed for the door. Then he was called back.

"Just one more thing, Giebenrath. You see quite a bit of Heilner, don't you?"

"Yes, quite a bit."

"More than of the others, I believe. Am I right?"

"But of course. He is my friend."

"But how did that happen? You are quite different from each other, aren't you?"

"I don't know. He's my friend, that's all."

"You know, don't you, that I don't much care for your friend. He is a restless, dissatisfied fellow; he may be gifted, but he does not accomplish much and does not have a good influence on you. It would make me glad if you saw a little less of him in the future. . . . Well?"

"I can't do that, sir."

"You can't? *Why* can't you?"

"Because he's my friend. I can't just leave him in the lurch like that."

"Hm. But you could make an attempt to spend a little more time with the others, couldn't you? You're the only one who gives in to Heilner's harmful influence like that, and the consequences are beginning to show. What is it that attracts you so much to him?"

"I don't know myself. But we care for each other and it would be low and cowardly of me to leave him like that."

"I see. Well, I won't force you. But I hope that you'll free yourself from him gradually. I would like that. I would like that very much."

These last words had none of his former mildness. Hans was free to go now.

From that day on, he slaved away but he no

longer made rapid progress as he used to. He had
his hands full just keeping pace and not falling behind. He himself was aware that his friendship
was partially responsible, but he regarded this not
as a loss or obstacle but a treasure worth everything he was missing in school—an intensified,
warmer form of existence to which his previous
sober and dutiful life could not hold a candle. He
was like someone in love for the first time: he
felt capable of performing great heroic deeds but
not the daily chore of boring, petty work. And
thus he forced himself back into the yoke again
and again with despairing sighs. He could not do
it like Heilner, who worked on the side and appro-
priated the most necessary things quickly and almost violently. Because his friend would call on
him almost every evening during their off-hours,
Hans forced himself to get up an hour earlier in
the morning and waged a bitter battle, especially
with his Hebrew grammar, as with a fiend. The
only work he still enjoyed was Homer and his
history lessons. Like a blind man feeling his way,
he neared an understanding of the Homeric world.
In history, the heroes stopped being mere names
with dates; they peered at him with burning eyes,
and each had living red lips and a face of his own.

Even while reading the Scriptures in Greek, he
was occasionally overwhelmed, even staggered, by
the distinctness and proximity of the figures. Once
in particular, while he read the sixth chapter of

Mark, where Jesus leaves his boat with the disciples, the words leaped up:

$$\epsilon \vartheta \vartheta \grave{v}s\ \grave{\epsilon}\pi\iota\gamma\nu\acute{o}\nu\tau\epsilon s\ a\grave{v}\tau\acute{o}\nu\ \pi\epsilon\rho\iota\acute{\epsilon}\delta\rho a\mu o\nu.$$

"Straightaway they knew him, they ran up to him." Then he too could see the Son of Man leaving the boat and recognized him at once—not by his figure or face but by the wide glowing depths of his loving eyes and by a gently beckoning or rather inviting and welcoming gesture of his beautiful, slender brown hands that seemed to be formed by the strong yet delicate soul that inhabited it. The edge of a turbulent lake and the bow of a heavy barque also appeared for a moment; then the entire picture vanished like a puff of breath in cold air.

At intervals something similar would happen and some personage or historical event would seemingly break forth hungrily from the books, yearning to live once more. Hans felt profoundly and strangely transformed by these fleeting apparitions, as though he had looked at the dark earth through a telescope or as though God had looked at him. These delicious moments were uncalled for, and vanished unlamented like pilgrims you do not dare speak to or friendly guests you dare not ask to stay because there's something alien and godly about them.

He kept these experiences to himself and did

not mention them to Heilner. The latter's previous melancholy had changed into a restless and biting intellectuality which criticized the monastery teachers, companions, the weather, human life in general and the existence of God, but occasionally would also lead to cantankerousness or silly impulsive pranks. Because Heilner lived in complete opposition to the rest of the students, Hans—who did nothing to oppose this—became just as disassociated from them. Hans felt fewer and fewer misgivings about this state of affairs as time went on. If only the headmaster, of whom he felt an obscure fear, were not there. After having been his favorite pupil, Hans was now being treated coolly and for obvious reasons neglected. For Hebrew especially, the headmaster's specialty, he had lost practically all enthusiasm.

It made for a delightful spectacle to observe how the forty new academy students had changed in body and soul in a matter of months, excepting a few whose growth seemed to have been arrested. Many had grown at a spectacular rate, much to the disadvantage of their physical bulk; their wrists and ankles stuck hopefully out of clothes which had not kept pace. The faces displayed the whole spectrum of shadings between vanishing childishness to budding manhood, and anyone who still lacked the angular forms of puberty had been lent a provisional manly seriousness, delicately wrinkled brows, from the study of the books of Moses. Chubby cheeks had actually become a rarity.

The less satisfied Hans was with his academic progress, the more resolutely did he—under Heilner's influence—cut himself off from his companions. No longer a model student and a potential first in class and therefore without cause to look down on anyone, his haughtiness did not suit him well. But he could not forgive his roommates for letting him know something of which he himself was acutely aware. He quarreled often, particularly with the well-mannered Hartner and the presumptuous Otto Wenger, and when the latter mocked and annoyed him one day Hans forgot himself and replied with his fists. A bloody fight ensued. Wenger was a coward but his weak opponent was easy game and he showed no mercy. Heilner was not there to help him. The rest of his roommates just watched and felt he had it coming. He received a regular beating, bled from the nose and all his ribs ached. He lay awake the entire night with shame, pain and anger. But he kept the incident secret from Heilner and only divorced himself even more rigorously from his roommates and from now on would hardly exchange a word with them.

Toward spring, under the influence of rainy afternoons, rainy Sundays and interminable dusks, new activities and movements began to flourish in the monastery. Acropolis, which counted a good pianist and two flute players in its midst, held two regularly scheduled musical evenings a week; Germania founded a dramatic reading group, and several young Pietists banded together and established a Bible-study circle and read a chapter every evening together with the appropriate commentary of the Calw Bible.

Heilner applied for membership in the dramatic group but was not accepted. He seethed with fury. As a form of revenge he now forced himself on the Bible group, where he wasn't wanted either, and his daring speeches and atheistic allusions aroused bitterness and wrangling in the modest little brotherhood. He soon tired of this game too, but retained an ironically Biblical tone of voice for some time after. However, no one paid him much heed, for the whole school was imbued with a spirit of adventure and enterprise.

A talented, witty fellow from Sparta caused the biggest stir. Apart from personal fame he was interested in bringing a little life into the old roost to break the monotony of their workaday routine. His nickname was Dunstan and he discovered an original way of creating a sensation and becoming a celebrity.

One morning as the boys came from their sleeping halls, they found a paper glued to the shower-room door, on which, under the heading of *Six Epigrams from Sparta*, a select number of the more unusual personalities—their foibles, escapades, friendships—were derided in rhyming couplets. The pair Giebenrath-Heilner received its blow too. An extraordinary uproar arose in the small community. The boys crowded around the bathroom door as though it were a theater entrance and the whole mob buzzed and pushed about like a swarm of bees when the queen is ready to take to the air.

The next morning the door literally prickled with epigrams, retorts, corroborations and new attacks, in which the instigator of the scandal had been shrewd enough to take no further part. He had achieved his purpose of setting the barn on fire; now he could sit back and watch the conflagration. For several days almost every boy joined in this war of epigrams. Lucius was probably the only one who went on with his work unperturbed as ever. Finally one of the teachers noticed what was up and put an end to this exciting game.

The shrewd Dunstan did not rest on his laurels; he had in the meantime prepared his master stroke. He now published the first issue of a newspaper which had been multigraphed in tiny format on exercise paper. He had been assembling material for weeks. It was called *Porcupine* and was primarily a satirical enterprise. A comical conversation between the author of the book of Joshua and a Maulbronn academy student was the prize feature of the first number. It had an enormous success and Dunstan, who now assumed the air of a busy editor-publisher, enjoyed almost as great and dubious a reputation as the famous Aretino in the republic of Venice.

General astonishment prevailed when Hermann Heilner took an enthusiastic share in the editing and joined with Dunstan in exercising the role of sharply satirical censor, a job for which he lacked neither wit nor venom. For about four weeks the little paper kept the whole monastery in a state of breathless excitement.

Hans had no objection to Heilner's participation. He himself lacked the talent as well as the inclination for it. At first he hardly noticed that Heilner spent so many evenings in Sparta; he was preoccupied with other things. During the day he walked about without energy and without paying much attention, worked with painful slowness and without pleasure. Then something peculiar happened to him during the Livy lesson.

The professor called on him to translate. He remained seated.

"What's the meaning of this? Why don't you stand up?" the professor exclaimed angrily.

Hans did not stir. He sat upright at his desk and held his head slightly lowered, with his eyes half-closed. The shout had half-roused him from his dreams, but the professor's voice seemed to come from a great distance. He felt his neighbor nudging him. But none of this mattered. He was surrounded by other people, other hands touched him and other voices talked to him; close, soft, deep voices that uttered no words but only a deep and soothing roar like an echoing well. And many eyes were gazing at him—alien, premonition-filled, great, glowing eyes. Perhaps they were the eyes of a crowd of Romans he had just been reading about in Livy, perhaps the eyes of unfamiliar people of whom he had dreamed or whom he had seen at one time in a painting.

"Giebenrath," the professor shouted, "are you asleep?"

The student slowly opened his eyes, stared in astonishment at the teacher and shook his head.

"Certainly you were asleep! Or can you tell me what sentence we are at? Well?"

Hans pointed to the sentence in the book. He knew very well where they were at.

"Do you think you could stand up?" the professor asked derisively. And Hans got up.

"What are you up to anyhow? Look at me!"

He looked at the professor. The professor did not care for the look. He shook his head as if puzzled.

"Are you feeling unwell, Giebenrath?"

"No, sir."

"Sit down and come to my room after class."

Hans sat down and looked at his Livy. He was wide awake and understood everything, but simultaneously his inner eye followed those many unfamiliar figures which were gradually receding into a great distance while always keeping their shining eyes fixed on him until they disappeared in a faraway mist. Simultaneously the teacher's voice and that of the student who was translating and all the other little noises of the schoolroom came closer and closer until they were finally as real and concrete as usual. Benches, lectern and blackboard were present as always; so were the big wooden compass and the wooden triangle on the wall, and his classmates, many of whom were stealing curious, unrestrained glances at him. Then Hans was startled; he heard someone say to him: "Come to my room after class." My God, what happened?

At the end of the lesson the professor gave him a sign to follow and they wound their way through the goggle-eyed students.

"Now tell me, what was the matter with you? You apparently were not asleep?"

"No, sir."

"Why didn't you get up when I asked you to?"

"I don't know."

"Or didn't you hear me? Are you hard of hearing?"

"No. I heard you."

"And you didn't get up? Afterwards you had such a strange look in your eyes. What were you thinking at the time?"

"Nothing. I wanted to get up."

"But why didn't you? So you didn't feel well after all?"

"I don't think I did. I don't know what it was."

"Did you have a headache?"

"No."

"It's all right. You can go now."

Just before supper he was called away again and taken to his sleeping quarters where he found the headmaster and the district doctor waiting for him. He was examined and questioned once more but nothing specific was discovered. The doctor laughed good-naturedly and made light of the matter.

"Those are slight nervous disorders, sir," he muttered half-jokingly to the headmaster, "a passing condition—light dizzy spells. You have to make sure that the young man gets a bit of fresh air every day. For his headaches I'll prescribe a few drops."

From then on Hans had to spend an hour in the open each day after supper. He had no objections. What was worse was that the headmaster had strictly forbidden Heilner to accompany him on these walks. Heilner cursed wildly but there was nothing he could do. Thus Hans went on these walks by himself and even liked them somewhat. It was the beginning of spring. The budding green swept like a thin bright wave over the evenly rounded hills; the trees shed their distinct wintry outlines in the interplay of the fresh young foliage and the green of the landscape which became a vast flowing tide of living green.

In his grammar-school days, Hans had looked at spring with a different eye, more with liveliness and curiosity and more attention to specific detail. He had observed the return of the migratory birds, one species after the other, and the sequence with which the trees began to blossom, and then, as soon as it was May, he had started to go fishing. Now he made no attempt to distinguish the dif-

ferent species of birds or recognize the bushes by
their buds. All he saw was the general activity,
the colors bursting forth everywhere; he breathed
in the smell of the young leaves, felt how much
softer and intoxicating the air was and walked
through the fields full of wonder. He tired easily
and always felt like lying down and sleeping. He
constantly saw other objects than those that
actually surrounded him. What they were he did
not really know himself and he did not give it
much thought. They were bright, delicate, unusual dreams which surrounded him like paintings
or like avenues lined with foreign trees that
seemed, however, devoid of life. Pure paintings,
only to be contemplated, but this contemplation
was a kind of experience too. It was being taken
and brought into another region, to other people.
It was wandering on alien grounds, or soft ground
on which it was a comfort to walk, and it was
breathing a strange air, an air full of lightness and
a delicate, dreamlike pungency. Occasionally, instead of these images there would come a feeling
—dark, warm, exciting—as though a gentle hand
were gliding caressingly over his body.

It was a great effort for Hans to concentrate
while reading and working. What failed to interest him vanished like a shadow under his hands.
If he wanted to remember his Hebrew vocabulary, he had to learn it during the last half-hour
before class. But often he had those moments when
he could see the physical presence of a descrip-

tion he had just read and could see it live and move much more vividly than his actual surroundings. And while he noticed with despair how his memory seemed unable to absorb anything new, and grew poorer and more untrustworthy from day to day, memories from earlier days would rush upon him with an ominous clarity that seemed both odd and disturbing. In the middle of a lesson or while reading he would suddenly find himself thinking of his father or old Anna, the housekeeper, or one of his former teachers or schoolmates: there they stood before him in the flesh, almost, and held his complete attention for a time. He also relived scenes from his stay in Stuttgart, from the examination and the vacation, over and over again, or would see himself sitting by the river with his fishing rod, smelling the sunwarmed water, and simultaneously it seemed to him as though the time of which he dreamed lay many many years in the past.

One damply tepid evening he was ambling back and forth through the dormitory hall with Heilner, telling him about his home, about his father, about going fishing and his school. His friend was noticeably quiet; he let him speak, gave a nod now and then and beat the air with his ruler a few times distractedly, the same ruler he played with all day long. Gradually Hans fell silent too; it had become night and they sat down on a window sill.

"You, Hans," Heilner finally began. His voice was unsure and excited.

"What is it?"

"Oh, nothing."

"No, go ahead."

"I just thought—because you told me some things about yourself—"

"What is it?"

"Tell me, Hans, didn't you ever run after a girl?"

There was a quiet spell. They had never talked about that. Hans was afraid of the subject, yet it attracted him magically. He could feel himself blushing now and his fingers trembled.

"Only once," he said in a whisper. "I was nothing but a boy at the time."

Another quiet spell.

"—and you, Heilner?"

Heilner sighed. "Oh, forget it! . . . You know one shouldn't talk about it, there's no point to it."

"But there is, there is!"

"I have a sweetheart."

"You? Really?"

"At home. The neighbor's girl. And this winter I gave her a kiss."

"You did?"

"Yes. . . . You know it was already dark. In the evening on the ice she let me help her take off her ice-skates. That's when I kissed her."

"Didn't she say anything?"

"Say anything? No. She just ran away."

"And then?"

"And then—nothing."

He sighed once more and Hans looked at him as if he were a hero who came from forbidden fields.

Then the bell rang and they had to go to bed. Once the lantern had been extinguished and it had become quiet, Hans lay awake for more than an hour thinking of the kiss Heilner had given his sweetheart.

The next day he wanted to find out more but felt ashamed to ask; and Heilner, because Hans did not ask him, was too shy to raise the subject on his own.

Hans' schoolwork went from bad to worse. The teachers began to look disgruntled and shot sour looks at him; the headmaster looked ominous and angry and his fellow students, too, had long since noticed how Hans had fallen from his previous height and was no longer aiming for first place. Only Heilner was not aware of anything unusual because schoolwork did not count for much with him. Hans watched all these events and changes without paying them any heed.

Heilner in the meantime had become fed up with working on the news sheet and again concentrated all his attention on his friend. As an act of stubborn defiance of the headmaster's edict, he accompanied Hans several times on his daily walk, lay in the sun with him and dreamed, read his poems aloud or cracked jokes about the headmaster. Hans still hoped that Heilner would continue with the revelation of his romantic adventures, yet the longer he desisted the less he could bring himself to inquire. Among the rest of the students both of them were as much disliked as ever, for Heilner's malicious barbs in *Porcupine* had not won him anyone's trust.

The newspaper was on its last legs anyway; it had outlived its function, which had been to bridge the uneventful weeks between winter and spring. Now the beginning of this beautiful season offered them more than enough entertainment with walks, identification of plants and outdoor games. Every afternoon, wrestlers, gymnasts, runners and ball players filled the cloister yard with screaming activity.

In addition there was a new *cause célèbre*. Its instigator—everybody's *bête noire*—was Hermann Heilner.

The headmaster, having heard that Heilner made light of his edict and accompanied Giebenrath on his walks almost every day, did not pick on Hans but asked the chief culprit, his old enemy, to come to his study. He called him by his first name, something which Heilner immediately protested. The headmaster reproached him for his disobedience. Heilner asserted he was Giebenrath's friend and no one had the right to forbid them to see each other. There resulted a real scene. Heilner was condemned to a few hours of house-arrest, and strictly prohibited from joining Giebenrath for the next few weeks.

Thus on the following day Hans once more took his official walk by himself. He returned at two o'clock and went into the classroom with the others. At the start of the lesson it developed that Heilner was absent. The situation was the same as when Hindu had disappeared. But this time no one thought that the absentee was delayed. At three o'clock the whole class and three teachers went out and patrolled the grounds for the missing boy. They separated into smaller groups, ran shouting about the woods, and some of them, including two teachers, did not think it inconceivable that Heilner had intentionally harmed himself.

At five o'clock all the police stations in the vicinity were alerted by telegram and in the evening a special-delivery letter was sent to Heilner's father. By late evening no trace of him had been found and the boys whispered in their sleeping quarters until late at night. The majority of them believed Heilner had drowned himself. Others felt that he'd simply gone home. But it had been ascertained that the runaway had no money.

Everybody looked at Hans as though he had to be in on the secret. But that was not the case. On the contrary, he was the most startled and miserable of the lot, and that night in the sleeping hall when he heard the others question, speculate, talk nonsense and crack jokes, he crept under his blan-

ket and lay awake hours in agony and fear for his
friend. He had a premonition he would not come
back and his heart was filled with woe until he
fell asleep from worry and exhaustion.

At just about that time Heilner was bedding down
in a wood only a few miles away. He was freezing
cold and could not fall asleep but he breathed
with a great feeling of relief and stretched his
limbs as though he had just escaped from a narrow cage. He had been on the road since noon,
had bought some bread in Knittlingen, and now
occasionally took a bite while glancing through the
sparsely covered sprigs at the dark night, the stars
and the swiftly moving clouds. It was all the same
to him where he would end up; what mattered
most was that he had finally escaped from the
hated monastery and shown the headmaster that his
will was stronger than mere commands and edicts.

All next day they looked for him, but in vain. He
spent his second night in a field near a village between bundles of straw. In the morning he re-
treated into the forest, and only toward evening,
as he was about to visit another village, was he
picked up by a gendarme. This man took charge
of him with friendly mockery and deposited him
at the city hall. There his wit and flattery won over
the mayor, who took him home for the night and
stuffed him with ham and eggs before putting him
to bed. Next day his father, who had arrived in the
meantime, came and fetched him.

The excitement was great at the monastery when

the runaway was brought back. But he kept his head high and did not seem to regret his brilliant little jaunt. The authorities demanded that he throw himself on their mercy. He refused, and in front of the teachers' tribunal he was neither timid nor subservient. They had wanted to keep him at the school but now his cup had run over. He was expelled in disgrace and in the evening he left with his father, never to return. He had been able to say good-bye to his friend Giebenrath only with a brief handshake.

The speech the headmaster delivered on the occasion of this extraordinary case of insubordination and degeneration was of singular beauty and verve. Much tamer, more factual and feebler was the report he sent to the school board in Stuttgart. All future correspondence with the expelled monster was prohibited, an edict which merely caused Hans Giebenrath to smile. For weeks Heilner and his flight were the main topic of conversation. The passage of time and his absence modified the general opinion of him and many looked back upon the fugitive, once so anxiously avoided, as an eagle escaped from captivity.

Hellas now contained two empty desks and the latter of the lost two students was not as quickly forgotten as the first. Yet the headmaster would have preferred to be certain that the second one would be just as peaceable and well taken care of. But Heilner did nothing to disturb the calm of the monastery. His friend waited and waited, but no letter came. He had vanished, and his physical appearance and his flight gradually became history and finally turned into legend. After many further brilliant escapades and misfortunes the passionate boy finally came into the strict discipline that a life of suffering can impose, and though he did not become a hero, he at least turned into a man.

The suspicion resting on Hans, of having known about Heilner's flight plans, cost him the rest of the teachers' goodwill. One of them said to him, when he could not answer a set of questions: "Why didn't you run off with that fine friend of yours?"

The headmaster no longer called on him in class and merely cast disdainful sidelong glances. Giebenrath no longer counted, he was one of the lepers.

Chapter Five

LIKE A HAMSTER, its cheeks distended by a store of provisions, Hans kept himself alive for a spell by drawing on his previously acquired knowledge. Then a painfully drawn-out death began, interrupted by brief ineffectual spurts whose utter futility made even Hans smile. He now stopped torturing himself uselessly, gave up on Homer and algebra as he had on the Pentateuch and on Xenophon, and watched with disinterest how his teacher's valuation sank step by step, from good to fair, from fair to satisfactory, and finally to zero. When he did not have a headache, which was rare, he thought of Hermann Heilner. Wide-eyed, he dreamed his lightheaded dreams and existed for hours on end as if he were only half-awake. To the growing annoyance of his teachers, he had recently begun to reply to them with a good-natured, humble smile. Wiedrich, a friendly young tutor, was the only one distressed at the sight of this smile and he treated the failing boy with sympathetic forbearance. The rest of the staff expressed indignation, punished Hans by not calling on him, or tried to rouse his sleeping ambition with occasional sarcasm.

"In case you're awake, might I trouble you to translate this sentence?"

The headmaster's state of indignation was nothing if not dignified. The vain man had the gift of the significant glance and was quite beside himself when Giebenrath countered his majestically threatening roll of the eyes with a meek, submissive smile. It finally got on the headmaster's nerves.

"Wipe the abysmally stupid smile from your face. You've more reason to weep."

A letter from Hans' father, beseeching him to improve, made a deeper impression. The headmaster's letter to Papa Giebenrath had frightened him out of his wits. His letter to Hans consisted of a collection of every encouraging and morally outraged cliché at the good man's disposal. It also revealed, though indirectly, a note of plaintive misery that distressed his son.

All these conscientious guides of youth—from the headmaster to Father Giebenrath, professors and tutors—regarded Hans as an impediment in their path, a recalcitrant and listless something which had to be compelled to move. No one, except perhaps Wiedrich, the sympathetic tutor, detected behind the slight boy's helpless smile the suffering of a drowning soul casting about desperately. Nor did it occur to any of them that a fragile creature had been reduced to this state by virtue of school and the barbaric ambition of his father and his grammar-school teacher. Why was he forced to work until late at night during the most sensitive and precarious period of his life? Why purposely alienated from his friends in grammar school? Why deprived of needed rest and forbidden to go fishing? Why instilled with a shabby ambition? Why had they not even granted him his well-deserved vacation after the examination?

Now the overworked little horse lay by the wayside, no longer of any use.

Toward summer the district doctor once more diagnosed Hans' difficulties as a nervous disorder, due principally to his growing. Hans was told to convalesce during vacation, eat well, run about the woods, and he would soon be better.

Unfortunately it never came to that. Three weeks before summer vacation Hans was given a sharp tongue-lashing by a professor during the afternoon lesson. While the professor shouted, Hans sank back in his bench, began to tremble and burst into a prolonged fit of weeping, disrupting the entire lesson. He spent the next half-day in bed.

The day following, he was asked during math class to draw a geometric figure on the board and demonstrate its proof. He stepped forward, but at the blackboard he felt dizzy, drew crazily with chalk and ruler, then dropped them and when he bent down to pick them up, he fell to the floor, unable to get up.

The district doctor was quite put out that his patient should indulge in such tricks. He ventured a cautious opinion, ordering an immediate sick-leave and calling in a nerve specialist. "That fellow will end up having St. Vitus's dance," he whispered to the headmaster, who nodded and found it expedient to change his facial expression from the previous ungracious angry look to a paternal and sympathetic one—something which came easily to him and fit him well.

He and the doctor each wrote a letter to Father Giebenrath, put them in the boy's pocket, and sent him home. Then the headmaster's anger changed to profound concern: what was the Stuttgart school board, so recently upset by the Heilner case, to think of this new misfortune? To everyone's astonishment he even dispensed with a lecture suitable to the occasion, and during Hans' last hours in school treated him with an almost ominous affability. It was self-evident to him that Hans would not return after his sick-leave; this student, who had fallen so far behind, could not possibly make up the weeks and months he had missed even if he recovered completely. Although he bade Hans a hearty good-bye with an encouraging, "I hope we'll see you back here soon," whenever he entered Hellas and caught sight of the three empty desks he felt a certain measure of embarrassment. He had trouble suppressing the thought that part of the blame for the disappearance of the two talented boys might yet be attached to him. But as he was a courageous and upright man, he eventually succeeded in dispelling these useless and gloomy doubts.

The monastery with its churches, gateway, gables and towers sank away behind the departing academician with his small suitcase; and in the place of woods and ranges of hills the fertile orchards of Baden's borderland appeared, then came Pforzheim and after that the first of the blue-black spruce-covered hills of the Black Forest, intersected by many valleys and streams. It seemed bluer and cooler, holding more than the usual promise of shady bliss. Hans contemplated the changing and increasingly familiar landscape with pleasure, until he drew near his home town; then he remembered his father, and a deep anxiety about his reception thoroughly ruined what little relief the trip home had afforded him. The trip to Stuttgart and the first trip to Maulbronn and all their expectation, excitement and anxiety came back to mind. What use had it all been? Like the headmaster, he realized that he would never return. This was the end of his academy days and of his studies, and all ambitious hopes. Yet the thought did not really sadden him now; only the fear of his disappointed father, whose hopes he had betrayed, weighed heavily on his heart. He longed for only one thing at present—to rest, to sleep, to cry, to dream as much as he wanted, to be left in peace. And he was afraid he would not be able to do this at home with his father. At the end of the trip, he had such a violent headache that he stopped looking out the window even though the train was passing through his favorite region, whose heights and forest he had roamed with such passion at one time. He almost failed to get off at the familiar railroad stop.

He stood there now, umbrella and suitcase in hand, while his father inspected him. The headmaster's last report had changed his disappointment and indignation into boundless fear. He had pictured Hans as hollow-cheeked and completely enfeebled; he found him looking thin and weak, but still walking on his own two legs. He felt a little easier now; but the worst thing was his secret dread of the nervous condition the headmaster and doctor had mentioned. No one in his family had ever suffered from nervous disorders. They always spoke of persons so afflicted with uncomprehending mockery or scornful pity, in the way they talked about lunatics. Now his own Hans was coming home with something like that.

The first day home the boy was glad to have been spared recriminations. Then he began to notice the shy and anxious care his father took of him with such obvious effort on his part. Occasionally he also became aware of his father casting peculiarly probing looks in his direction, regarding him with an unholy curiosity and speaking to him in a muted hypocritical tone of voice, observing him only when he thought Hans would not notice. The upshot of this was that Hans became even more timid; a vague fear of his own condition began to torment him.

When the weather was fine, he would lie for hours in the forest—and he felt soothed by this. A pale shadow of his former boyhood bliss touched his injured soul: pleasure in flowers and in insects, in observing birds or tracking animals. But this was short-lived. Most of the time he stretched out listless in the moss, suffered from headaches and vainly tried to think of something until daydreams returned to transport him into another realm.

Once he had a dream. He saw his friend Heilner, laid out on a stretcher. When he tried to approach, the headmaster and the teachers kept pushing him back, and whenever he advanced, they gave him short, painful jabs. The professors and tutors from the academy were not his only tormentors—the principal of the school and the Stuttgart examiners were also among them, all with embittered countenances. Suddenly the scene changed and the drowned Hindu lay on the stretcher, his comical father in his high top hat standing bowlegged by his side.

There was another dream. He was running in the forest looking for Heilner. He kept spotting him at a great distance among the trees but whenever he was about to shout his name he saw him disappear. Finally Heilner stopped, let him approach and then said: "Hey, you know, I have a sweetheart." Then he broke out into a terribly loud laugh and disappeared in the undergrowth.

In the same dream he saw a slim and handsome man alight from a boat, with tranquil, godlike eyes and peaceful hands, and he ran up to him. The scene dissolved and he tried to remember what it meant until the sentence in Mark came back to him:

$$εὐθὺς ἐπιγνόντες αὐτὸν περιέδραμον.$$

"Straightaway they knew him, they ran up to him." Now he had to remember what form

$$περιέδραμον$$

was and what the present tense, infinitive, perfect and future of the verb were. He had to conjugate it in the singular, dual and plural, and he began to panic whenever he got stuck. When he came to himself again, he felt as if his head were sore inside. When his face involuntarily took on his old guilty and resigned smile, he instantly heard the headmaster say: "Wipe that grin from your face."

All in all, Hans' condition showed little improvement despite the few days during which he felt better. On the contrary, everything was still going downhill with him. The family doctor, who had treated his mother and pronounced her dead and who attended his father when he came down with gout, pulled a long face and put off making a diagnosis from one day to the next.

During these weeks Hans realized for the first time that he had had no friends during his last two years in grammar school. Some of his former companions had left town altogether, and others, he noticed, had become apprentices. With none of them did he have anything in common, there was nothing he wanted from any of them, and none of them bothered with him. His old principal twice addressed a few friendly words to him. The Latin teacher and the pastor would give him a friendly nod when they met him on the street, but Hans was no longer any concern of theirs. He was no longer a vessel which could be stuffed with all sorts of things, no longer fertile ground for a variety of seeds; he was no longer worth their time and effort.

Perhaps it would have helped him if the pastor had shown some interest in him. But what should the pastor have done? What he was in a position to give—knowledge, or at least the incentive to search for it—he had not withheld from the boy, and that was all he had to give. He was not one of those pastors whose competence in Latin is in doubt and whose sermons are drawn from well-known sources, but to whom you gladly turn in troubled times because of their kind eyes and the friendly words they have for all who suffer. Nor was Papa Giebenrath a friend or consoler, even if he made an effort to conceal his anger and disappointment from Hans.

Thus the boy felt abandoned, unloved; he sat around in the small garden sunning himself, or lay in the woods and gave himself up to his dreams or tormenting thoughts. He was unable to find solace in reading because his eyes and head would begin to hurt as soon as he opened a book, and the ghost of his days at the academy and all his fears would return to haunt him, filling him with dreadful dreams during which he felt as if he were choking and being riveted by burning eyes.

In these desperate and forlorn straits, another ghost approached the sickly boy in the guise of a treacherous comforter that gradually became familiar and indispensable: the thought of death. It was easy enough to obtain a gun or to attach a noose to a tree somewhere in the forest. The thought of death accompanied him on his daily walks. He inspected various quiet, lonely places until he finally chose one where it would be good to die. He designated this as the place where he would definitely end his life. He visited it time and again, and sitting there derived peculiar pleasure from imagining how they would soon find his corpse there. He not only chose a branch for the rope but had tested it—no further obstacles stood in his way. Little by little he composed a brief farewell letter to his father and a much longer one to Hermann Heilner. They were to be found on his corpse.

These preparations with their sense of purpose-fulness exerted a beneficial influence on his state of mind. Sitting under the fateful branch, he enjoyed many hours during which the pressure lifted from him and a feeling of almost joyous well-being overcame him.

He did not really know why he hadn't hanged himself long ago. His mind was made up, he had passed the death sentence on himself, and this made him feel so well that in the meantime he did not scorn—in these his last days—the enjoyment of sunshine and his solitary dreams in the way you do before setting out on a long trip. He could leave any day he chose, everything was settled. And he took particular and bitter satisfaction in lingering voluntarily for a while in his old surroundings, looking into the faces of people who had no idea of his dangerous resolve. Whenever he encountered the doctor, he could not help thinking: "Well, my friend, I'd almost like to be around to see the face you'll make."

Fate allowed him to enjoy his gloomy intentions. She watched him every day sipping a few drops of joy and zest from the cup of death. There might be precious little in store for this crippled young being, but nonetheless it must complete its appointed course and not leave this earth before having drunk a little deeper of life's bitter-sweet waters.

Inescapable, oppressive images haunted him less and less frequently. He gave way to a weary feeling of capitulation, a painless and listless mood in which he saw hours and days pass, gazed blandly into the blue sky. At times he seemed to be sleepwalking; at others he seemed to be returning to childhood. Once he sat beneath the spruce in their little garden, enveloped in a lazy twilit mood, and hummed, without being aware of it, the same old verses over and over to himself, verses he remembered from his grammar-school days:

> *"Oh, I am so weary*
> *Oh, I am so weak*
> *Have no money in my wallet*
> *And nothing in my satchel."*

He hummed it in the old accustomed manner and thought nothing of repeating the same verse twenty times over. But his father happened to be listening near the window, and was shocked. This pleasant and mindless singsong was beyond his sober sensibility; he interpreted it, with a deep sigh, as a sign of hopeless mental decline. From that day on he watched his son even more anxiously. And his son, of course, noticed and suffered from this. Yet Hans still could not find the right moment to take the rope to the forest and put that strong branch to good use.

Meanwhile the hottest time of year had set in, and now twelve months had passed since the examination and the summer holidays which followed. Every so often Hans thought back to those events, but without feeling any particularly strong emotion; he had become quite insensitive. He would have liked to go fishing again but dared not ask his father for permission. Yet whenever he came near the water and stood any length of time in a place where no one could see him, his eyes eagerly followed the movement of the dark, noiseless fish as they swam about; it was agony to realize that he could not go fishing.

Every day toward evening he walked a stretch downriver to go swimming. Because he always had to pass by Inspector Gessler's little house he discovered by chance the return of Emma Gessler, on whom he had such a crush three years ago. He cast a curious eye at her a few times, but he no longer much cared for her. She had been a finely built delicate girl at that time; now she had grown heavy, her movements were angular, her modern hairdo looked far too adult and disfigured her completely. Nor did long dresses suit her, and her attempt to look ladylike was decidedly unfortunate. Hans found her ridiculous but at the same time he felt sorry for her when he remembered how peculiarly sweet and dark and warm he had felt whenever he had seen her. Indeed, everything had been completely different, so much more beautiful, so much livelier! It had been such a long time since he had known anything but Latin, history, Greek, examinations, academy and headaches. In those days his books contained fairy tales, cops and robbers. The mill he had constructed in the garden had been running and in the evening he had listened to Liese tell her wild stories in the gateway of Naschold's house. At that time he had regarded his old neighbor Grossjohann, nicknamed Garibaldi, as a murderer and robber and had dreamed of him. Throughout the year he had always looked forward to something or other every month: hay-making, clover-mowing, the first day you could go fishing, catch crayfish, pick hops, shake plums off the trees, burn weeds in potato fields, and the first day of threshing. In between there had been Sundays and holidays. There had been so many things that mysteriously attracted him: houses, little alleys, haylofts, wells, fences; people and animals of every kind had been familiar and dear to him or fascinating. When he had gone hops-picking he listened to the older girls and memorized some of the verses they sang, most of them light and funny but a few oddly sorrowful.

All of that had come to an end without his even noticing it. First the evenings with Liese had been no more, then fishing for minnows on Sunday mornings, then the reading of fairy tales and so on, one thing after the other, including hops-picking and the mill in the garden. Where had it all gone?

And what happened was that the precocious boy experienced an unreal second childhood during this period of illness. His sensibility, robbed of its real childhood, now fled with sudden yearning back to those already dimming years and wandered spellbound through a forest of memories whose vividness was perhaps of an almost pathological nature. He relived these memories with no less intensity and passion than he had experienced them in reality before. His betrayed and violated childhood erupted like a long pent-up spring.

When a tree is polled, it will sprout new shoots nearer its roots. A soul that is ruined in the bud will frequently return to the springtime of its beginnings and its promise-filled childhood, as though it could discover new hopes there and retie the broken threads of life. The shoots grow rapidly and eagerly, but it is only a sham life that will never be a genuine tree.

This is what was happening to Hans Giebenrath, so let us accompany him into his childhood land of dreams.

The Giebenrath house stood near the old stone bridge on a corner between two entirely different streets. The first of these streets, to which the house actually belonged, was the longest, widest, most dignified in town. It was called Tannery Street. The second street led up a steep hill, was short, narrow and miserable; it was named Falcon after an age-old inn that had long since been shut down, whose sign had displayed a falcon.

In house after house on Tannery Street there lived good, solid, well-established families, people who owned their own houses, had their own pews in church, whose gardens rose in terraces steeply uphill and whose fences, all overgrown with yellow broom, bordered on the railroad right-of-way that had been laid out in the 1870's. For splendor and respectability, nothing could compare with Tannery Street except the town square, where church, courthouse, county administration, town hall and vicarage were situated with unalloyed dignity and lent this little town a certain nobility, the illusion of being a city. Tannery Street, though lacking such official attributes, consisted of old and new middle-class dwellings with impressive doors, old-fashioned half-timbered houses with brightly decorated gables. The entire street exuded a friendly atmosphere of well-lighted comfort, due in large part to the fact that it consisted of a single row of houses. The other side of the street was open, save for a wall, propped up by wooden pilings, behind which the river flowed.

If Tannery Street was long, wide and spaciously dignified, Falcon was the opposite. Here stood warped gloomy houses with splotched and crumbling plaster, gables that lurched forward, broken and often patched windows and doors, crooked chimneys, leaky rain pipes. The houses deprived each other of room and light and the little alley was narrow, oddly twisted and cast in a perpetual gloom which rainstorms or dusk changed into damp darkness. Masses of wash always hung on lines and poles outside the windows. As small and miserable as the street was, hordes of people made their homes here, not even counting the sub-tenants and those who flopped there for the night. Every nook and cranny of these ill-shaped, aging houses was occupied. The street was densely populated and poverty, vice and sickness were rank. If a typhus epidemic broke out, it would start here; if manslaughter were to occur, it would be here, and if something was stolen in town people looked first in the Falcon. Peddlers had their lodgings there, among whom were Hottehotte, the queer vendor of silver polish and Adam Hittel, the scissors grinder, a man accused of every imaginable crime and vice.

During his first years in school Hans had been a frequent visitor in the Falcon. In the company of a dubious gang of flaxen-haired, ragged boys he had listened to the notorious Lotte Frohmüller's tales of murder. She was divorced from a small innkeeper and had spent five years in prison. She had been a well-known beauty in her day, had had any number of lovers among the factory workers, and caused any number of scandals and knife fights. Now she lived alone and spent her evenings, after the factory closed, making coffee and telling stories. Her door was always open and besides the wives and young workers a horde of neighborhood children listened from the doorstep with a mixture of delight and terror. The water in the kettle boiled on the black stone hearth, a tallow candle burned nearby. It added its adventurous flickering to the blue flame from the little coal fire; together they illuminated the overcrowded dark room and cast hugely enlarged shadows of the listeners on walls and ceilings, filling the room with ghostly activity.

Hans made his first acquaintance with the brothers Finkenbein at the age of eight and remained friends with them for almost a year, despite his father's strict prohibition. Dolf and Emil Finkenbein were the sharpest street boys in town. Famous for stealing cherries and apples and minor transgressions against the forestry laws, they were also expert in all kinds of tricks and pranks. On the side they conducted a flourishing trade in bird eggs, lead pellets, young ravens, starlings and rabbits, and transgressed a town ordinance by leaving baited lines in the river overnight. They felt at home in every garden in town, for no fence was too sharply pointed, no wall so thickly crowned with broken glass that they could not easily scale it.

Hans had become an even closer friend of Hermann Rechtenheil, who also lived in the Falcon. He was an orphan, a sickly, precocious and unusual child. Because one of his legs was shorter than the other, he could only hobble with the help of a stick and took no part in the street games. He was of slight build and had a pale, ailing face with a mouth prematurely bitter and a chin that was excessively pointed. He was an exceptionally dexterous and enthusiastic angler, a passion he communicated to Hans. Hans did not have a fishing license at that time but they went anyway, secretly, to out-of-the-way spots. If hunting is a pleasure, then poaching, as everyone knows, is a supreme delight. The hobbled Rechtenheil taught Hans to pick the right rods, pleat horsehair, dye his lines, tie running knots and sharpen fishhooks. He taught him to watch for telltale weather signs, to observe the water and muddy it with white clay, select the right bait for fastening to his hook; he also taught him to distinguish the various kinds of fish, to listen for the fish and to keep the line at the proper depth. By wordless example he communicated to Hans the delicate sense of when to pull in or let out the line. He vociferated against store-bought rods, floats and transparent lines and all other artificial paraphernalia, and he convinced Hans that there was no real fishing with tackle whose parts you had not put together yourself.

Hans and the Finkenbein brothers had gone their separate ways after an angry quarrel. Hans' friendship with the quiet, lame Rechtenheil ended on a different note. One day in February his friend crawled into a miserable little bed, after laying his crutch across his clothes on the chair, and passed away quickly and quietly; the Falcon forgot him immediately and only Hans cherished his memory for long.

But this death by no means exhausted the fund of odd people that inhabited the Falcon. Who for instance didn't know Rötteler, the former postman, fired for being an alcoholic, who now lay every week or so in the gutter, the cause of endless nightly uproars but otherwise as gentle as a child, always beaming with goodwill? He had given Hans a sniff from his oval snuffbox, accepted an occasional fish from him, fried them in butter and invited Hans to lunch. He was the proud owner of a stuffed buzzard with glass eyes, of an old music box that played old-fashioned dances in thin, delicate tones. And who for instance didn't know Porsch, the overaged mechanic, who always wore a tie even when he went barefoot? As the son of a strict rural teacher of the old school he knew half the Bible by heart and could stuff your ears with sayings and moral aphorisms. But neither his tendency to moralize nor his snow-white hair kept him from flirting with all the girls or getting soused regularly. When he was good and high he liked to sit on the curb by the Giebenrath house, addressing everyone by first names and showering them with proverbs.

"Hans Giebenrath, my good son, pray listen to what I have to tell thee! How sayeth Ecclesiasticus? 'Blessed is the man that has not sinned with his mouth and whose conscience hath not condemned him. As of the green leaves on a thick tree, some fall and some grow; so is the generation of flesh and blood, one cometh to an end and another is born.' Well, now be off with you, you old scoundrel."

In spite of all his Christian utterances, old Porsch was full of terrifying legends about ghosts and the like. He was familiar with the places they haunted and always teetered between belief and disbelief in his own stories. Generally he would launch one of them in an uncertain, boastful tone of voice, mocking both story and listener, but during the process of narration he began to hunch forward anxiously; his voice lost more and more volume and in the end became an insistent, uncanny whisper.

What a number of ominous, obscurely alluring things this wretched little street contained! Locksmith Brendly lived there after his business failed, after his disheveled workshop went completely to pot. He sat half the day at his little window, gazing grimly out at the bustling alley; occasionally when one of the filthy, ragged neighborhood children fell into his hands, he tortured it in a fit of malicious glee, pulled its ears and hair and pinched it until its whole body was black and blue. Yet one day he was found hanging from his banister on a piece of zinc wire, looking so hideous that no one dared come near him until old Porsch, the mechanic, cut the wire with metal shears from behind, whereupon the corpse, tongue protruding, plunged head over heels down the stairs into the midst of the horrified spectators.

Every time Hans stepped from the well-lighted broad Tannery Street into the dank darkness of Falcon, its peculiarly cloying air caused a marvelously gruesome sense of oppression, a mixture of curiosity, dread, bad conscience and blissful intimation of adventure. The Falcon was the only place where a fairy tale, a miracle or an unspeakable act of horror might happen, where magic and ghosts were credible, even likely, and where you could experience the very same painfully delicious shudder that comes with reading sagas, or the scandalous *Reutlinger Folk Tales*, which teachers confiscate and which recount the wicked deeds and punishments of villains like Sonnenwirtle, Schinderhannes, the Postmichel, Jack-the-Ripper and similar sinister heroes, criminals and adventurers.

Apart from the Falcon there was one other place where you could experience and hear unusual things, become lost in dark lofts and strange rooms. That was the nearby tannery, the huge old building where the animal hides hung in the twilit lofts, where the cellars contained hidden covers and forbidden tunnels and where in the evening Liese often told her wonderful stories to all the children. What transpired at the tannery was friendlier and calmer, more human than in the Falcon, but no less mysterious. The work the tanners performed in the various holes, in the cellar, in the tannery yard and on the clay floors seemed strange and unintelligible. The vast rooms were as quiet and as intriguing as they were ominous; the powerfully built and ill-tempered master was shunned and dreaded like a cannibal, and Liese went about this remarkable building like a good fairy, a protector and mother to all children, birds, cats and little dogs, the embodiment of goodness, fairy tales and songs.

Hans' thoughts and dreams now moved in this world to which he had been so long a stranger. He sought refuge from his great disappointment and hopelessness in a past that had been good to him. In those days he had been full of hope, had seen the world lying before him like a vast enchanted forest holding gruesome dangers, accursed treasures and emerald castles in its impenetrable depths. He had entered a little way into this wilderness but he had become weary before he had found miracles. Now he stood once more before the mysteriously twilit entrance, as an exile whose curiosity was futile.

Hans went back to the Falcon a few times and found there the familiar dankness and vile odors, the old nooks and lightless stairwells. Hoary men and women still sat about on doorsteps, and unwashed, flaxen-haired children ran around yelling. Porsch, the mechanic, looked older than ever, no longer recognized Hans and replied to his timid greeting with derisive cackling. Grossjohann, nicknamed Garibaldi, had died, as had Lotte Frohmüller. Rötteler, the mailman, still existed. He complained that the boys had ruined his music box, proffered his snuffbox and then tried to touch Hans for a few pennies; finally he told about the brothers Finkenbein—one of them worked at the cigar factory and was drinking as heavily as his old man; the other had fled after being involved in a knife fight at a church bazaar and had not been heard of or seen for a year. All that made a pitiful impression on Hans.

One evening Hans went over to the tannery. Something seemed to draw him through the gateway and across the damp yard as though his childhood and all its vanished joys lay hidden in the huge old building.

After walking up the uneven steps and across the cobblestone court, he came to the dark stairway and groped his way to the clay court where the hides were stretched to dry: there with the pungent smell of the leather he inhaled a whole world of resurgent memories. He climbed down again and looked into the backyard that contained the tannery pits and the high, narrow-roofed frames for dying tanner's bark. Liese sat at her appointed spot on the bench by the wall, a basket full of potatoes in front of her, and a few children around her, listening.

Hans stopped in the dark doorway and cocked his ear in her direction. A great sense of peace filled the twilit tanner's garden. Apart from the soft rushing sound the river made as it flowed past, behind the wall, all there was to hear was the soft rasping of Liese's knife against the potatoes and her voice, telling stories. The children sat or crouched calmly and hardly moved. She was recounting the tale of St. Christopher, whom a child's voice called across the stream at night.

Hans listened for a while. Then he walked slowly back through the courtyard and home. He felt that he could not become a child again after all and sit beside Liese, and from now on he avoided the tannery as much as the Falcon.

Chapter Six

FALL HAD LEFT its marks: isolated beech trees and birches held yellow and red torches among the dark spruces. Fog hovered in the ravines for longer periods, and the river steamed in the mornings.

Hans, the pale ex-academician, still roamed the countryside each day. He felt listless and unhappy and avoided what little company he could have had. The doctor prescribed drops, cod liver oil, eggs and cold showers.

No wonder that none of this helped. Every healthy person must have a goal in life and that life must have content; young Giebenrath had lost both. His father now concluded that Hans should become a clerk or be apprenticed to some craftsman. But the boy was still weak and needed to regain more of his strength. Even so, the time had come to get serious with him.

Since the first bewildering impressions had receded and since he no longer believed in committing suicide, Hans had drifted from his hysterically unpredictable state of fear into one of uniform melancholy into which he sank deeper slowly and helplessly as if in a bog.

Now he roamed the autumnal fields and succumbed to the influence of that season. The decline of the year in silently falling leaves, the fading of the meadows in the dense early morning fog and the ripe, weary yearning for death of all vegetation induced in Hans, as in all sick persons, a receptivity to melancholy and despair. He felt the desire to sink down, to fall asleep, to die, and suffered agonies because his youth itself made this impossible, clinging to life with its quiet obstinacy.

He watched the trees turn yellow, brown, bare; the milk-white fog rise like smoke out of the forests and gardens where all life has died out after the last fruits are picked but in which no one paid heed to the colorfully fading asters. He watched fallen leaves cover the river where no one fished or swam any more, whose cold edge was left to the tanners alone.

During the last few days masses of apple-pulp had been floating down-river. People were busy making cider and the fragrance of fermenting fruit juice could be smelled all over town.

In the mill, which was furthest downstream, shoemaker Flaig had rented a small cider press and invited Hans to help him with the work.

The yard in front of the mill was covered with cider presses, large and small, with carts, baskets and sacks full of fruit, with tubs, vats, barrels, whole mountains of brown apple-pulp, wooden levers, wheelbarrows, empty carts. The presses labored, crunched, squeaked, groaned and bleated. Most of them were lacquered green, and this green along with the yellowed pulp, the colors of the fruit in baskets, the light green river, the barefoot children and the clear autumn sun made on everyone witnessing this scene an impression of joy, zest and plenty. The crunching of the apples sounded harsh but appetizing. Anyone passing by who heard this sound could not help reaching for an apple and taking a bite. The sweet cider poured out of the pipes in a thick stream, reddish-yellow, sparkling in the sun. Anyone passing by who saw this could not help asking for a glass, taking a sip and then just standing there, his eyes moistened by a sense of well-being and sweetness which surged through him. And this sweet cider filled the air far and wide with its delicious fragrance.

This fragrance really was the best part of the year, for it is the very essence of ripeness and harvest. It is good to suck it into your lungs with winter so near since it makes you grateful and brings back a host of memories: of the gentle May rains, summer downpours, cool morning dew in autumn, tender spring sun, blazing hot summer afternoons, the whites and rose-red blossoms and the ripe red-brown glow of fruit trees before the harvest—everything beautiful and joyful that happens in the course of a year.

Those were marvelous days for everyone. The ostentatiously rich, inasmuch as they condescended to appear in person, weighed a juicy apple in one hand, counted their half-dozen or more sacks, sampled their cider with a silver beaker and made sure everyone heard how not a single drop of water weakened it. The poor brought only one sack full of apples, sampled their cider with a glass or an earthenware dish, added water and were no less proud or happy. Those unable to make their own cider ran from one acquaintance and neighbor's press to the other, received a glassful of cider and an apple from all of them and demonstrated by way of expert commentary that they knew their part of the business too. All the children, rich and poor, ran about with little beakers, each clutching a half-eaten apple and a hunk of bread, for, according to an old but unfounded legend, if you ate enough bread while drinking new cider you would avoid an upset stomach.

Hundreds of voices yelled and screamed at the same time, that is, apart from the racket the children made, and all these noises contributed to a busy, excited and cheerful hubbub.

"Hey, Hannes, come here! Over here. Just one glassful."

"Thanks, thanks. I've the runs already."

"What d'you pay for the hundredweight?"

"Four marks. But they're great. Here, have a sip."

Occasionally a small mishap occurred. A sack of

apples would burst and the apples would roll into the dirt.

"Dammit, my apples! Help me, you people!"

Everyone would help pick up the spilled apples and only a few little punks would take advantage of the situation.

"Keep 'em out of your pockets! Stuff yourselves but not your pockets. Just watch it, Gutedel, you clumsy oaf!"

"Hi there, neighbor! You needn't be so stuck up. Come, have a taste."

"It's like honey! Exactly like honey. How much are you making?"

"Two kegs full, that's all, but it won't be the worst!"

"It's a good thing we don't press in midsummer or all of it would be drunk up by now."

This year too a few disgruntled old folks were present. They had not pressed their own cider for years but kept telling you about the year so-and-so when apples were so plentiful you could practically have them for nothing. Everything had been so much cheaper and better, no one had even thought of adding sugar in those days, and anyway there was just no comparison between what the trees bore then and now.

"Those were the harvests! I had an apple tree that threw down its five-hundred weight all by its own self."

But as bad as the times were, the disgruntled oldsters were not lax to sample the cider, and those who still had teeth were all gnawing at apples. One of them had even forced down so many apples he had gotten a miserable case of heartburn.

"As I said," he reasoned, "I used to eat ten of 'em." And with undissembling sighs he thought upon the time when he could eat ten large apples before he got heartburn.

Master Flaig's cider press stood in the middle of this throng. His senior apprentice lent a hand. Flaig obtained his apples from the Baden region and his cider was always of the best. He was quietly happy and stopped no one from taking his little "taste." His children were even more cheerful; they scurried about letting themselves be carried away with the throng. But the most cheerful of all, even if he did not show it, was his apprentice. He came from a poor farmhouse up in the forest. He was glad to be in the open air again and to work up a good sweat; the good sweet cider also agreed with him. His healthy farmboy's face grinned like a satyr's mask; his shoemaker's hands were cleaner than on Sundays.

When Hans Giebenrath first reached this area, he was subdued and afraid; he had not come gladly. But right away, at the first cider press he passed, he was given a beakerful, and from Naschold's Liese of all people. He took a sip, and while he swallowed the sweet strong cider, its taste brought back any number of smiling memories of bygone autumns and filled him with the timid yearning to join the frolicking again for a change and to have a good time. Acquaintances talked to him, glasses were proffered, and when he reached Flaig's press, the general festivity and drinking had taken hold of him and begun to transform him. He tossed the shoemaker a snappy greeting and cracked a few of the customary cider jokes. The master hid his astonishment and bade him a cheerful welcome.

Half an hour had passed when a girl in a blue skirt approached, gave Flaig and the apprentice a bright laugh and began helping them.

"Well, yes," said the shoemaker, "that's my niece from Heilbronn. Of course she's used to a different kind of harvest what with all the vineyards where she lives."

She was about eighteen or nineteen years old, agile and gay, not tall but well built and with a good figure. Her warm dark eyes shone cheerful and intelligent in her round face with its pretty, kissable mouth. Although she certainly looked like a healthy and lively Heilbronn girl, she did not in the least give the impression of being a relative of the devout shoemaker. She was very much of this world and her eyes did not look like the kind that are glued to the Bible at night.

Hans suddenly began to look unhappy again and wished fervently that Emma would soon leave. But she stayed on and laughed and sang and chattered away and knew a quick comeback to every joke. Hans felt ashamed and became completely quiet. Having to deal with young girls

whom he had to call "Miss" he found awful anyway. This one was so lively and talkative, she
paid no attention to him or his shyness, so he
withdrew his feelers awkwardly and a little offended and crawled back into himself like a snail
brushed by a cartwheel. He kept quiet and tried
to look like someone who is bored; but he did not
succeed and instead wore a face as though there
had been a death in the family.

No one had time to notice any of this, Emma
least of all. As Hans found out, she had been
visiting the Flaigs for the last two weeks but she
already knew the whole town. She ran from
rich to poor, tasted the new cider, kidded everyone,
laughed a little, came back, pretended to help,
picked up the children, gave away apples and
created an abundance of laughter and joy around
her. She called out to every child that passed:
"Want an apple?" Then she would select a fine
red one, place her hands behind her back and let
them guess: "Left or right?" But the boys never
guessed what hand the apple was in, and only when
they started to shout did she give them an apple
but always a smaller, greener one. She also seemed
well informed about Hans and asked him whether
he was the one who always had the headaches,
but even before he could answer she was talking
to someone else.

Hans was of a mind to quit and go home when
Flaig placed the lever in his hand.

"So, now you can work a while, Emma'll help you. I've got to go back to the shop."

The master left, leaving the apprentice to help his wife cart off the cider kegs, and Hans and Emma to tend the press. Hans clenched his teeth and worked like a fiend.

When he began to wonder why the lever was so difficult to push, he looked up and the girl burst into bright laughter. She had been leaning against it as a joke and when Hans furiously tried to pull it up she did it again.

He didn't say a word. But while he pushed the lever with the girl's body leaning against it on the other side, he suddenly felt quite inhibited; gradually he stopped trying to turn the lever. A sweet fear overcame him. When the young slip of a thing laughed cheekily directly into his face she suddenly seemed transformed, more of a friend yet less familiar, and now he too laughed a little laugh of awkward intimacy.

And then the lever came to a complete stop.

And Emma said: "Let's not kill ourselves," and handed him the half-full glass from which she had just drunk.

This mouthful of cider seemed much sweeter and more powerful than the last, and when he had emptied the glass, he looked longingly at it and wondered why his heart beat so swiftly and he breathed with such difficulty.

Then they worked again for a while. He didn't really know what he was doing when he placed himself in such a way that the girl's skirt had to brush him and his hand touched hers, and whenever this happened his heart would seemingly come to a stop with anxious bliss and a pleasantly sweet weakness came over him.

He did not know what he was saying but he answered all her questions, laughed when she laughed, wagged his finger at her a few times when she fooled around and twice more emptied a glass from her hand. At the same time a whole swarm of memories rushed through his mind; servant girls he had seen standing with their boyfriends in doorways, a few sentences from novels, the kiss Heilner had given him, and a mass of words, stories and dark hints dropped during schoolboy conversations about the "girls" and "what it's like if you have a sweetheart."

Everything was transformed. The isolated voices, curses and laughter merged into an indistinguishable curtain of noise; the river and the old bridge looked remote as if painted on canvas.

Emma also looked different. He no longer saw her entire face—just her dark happy eyes and her red mouth, sharp white teeth; a slipper with a black stocking above it, then a handful of curls dangling loosely in the back of her neck, a round tanned neck gliding into a blue bodice, the firm shoulders and the heaving breasts underneath, a pink translucent ear.

And after another while she let her beaker drop into the vat, and when she bent down for it, she pressed her knee against his wrist at the side of the vat. And he too bent down but more slowly and almost brushed his face against her hair. The hair gave off a weak scent and beneath it in the shadow of loose curls there glowed a warm, tanned, beautiful neck that disappeared into the blue bodice through whose tightly stretched lacing he caught a glimpse of the back of her waist.

When he straightened up again and her knee touched his hand and her hair grazed his cheek, he saw that she was flushed from bending down, and a tremor passed through all his limbs. He turned pale and for a moment felt such a profound weariness that he had to steady himself by holding on to the press. His heart quivered, his arms became weak and his shoulders ached.

From that moment on he hardly said another word and avoided her gaze. However, as soon as she looked away, he stared at her with a mixture of unfamiliar desire and bad conscience. In this hour something broke inside him and a new, alien but enticing land with distant blue shores opened up before his soul. He did not know or could only guess what the apprehension and sweet agony signified, and did not know which was stronger, pain or desire.

But the desire signified the victory of his adolescent vigor and sensuality and the first intimation of the mighty forces of life, and the pain signified that the morning peace had been broken, that his

soul had left that childhood land which can never
be found again. His small fragile ship had barely
escaped a near disaster; now it entered a region of
new storms and uncharted depths through which
even the best-led adolescent cannot find a trustworthy guide. He must find his own way and be
his own savior.

It was a good thing that the apprentice came
back and relieved him at the press. Hans stayed on
for a while, hoping for one more touch or a
friendly word from Emma, who was again chattering away with people at other cider presses. But
because Hans felt embarrassed in front of the apprentice, he slipped off without saying good-bye.

It was remarkable how everything had changed,
how beautiful and exciting it had become. The
starlings which had fattened up on the apple-pulp
shot noisily through a sky that had never looked
as high and beautiful, as blue and yearning. Never
had the river looked like such a pure, blue-green
mirror, nor had it held such a blindingly white
roaring weir. All this seemed a decorative newly
painted picture behind clear new glass. Everything
seemed to await the beginning of a great feast. He
himself felt a strong, sweet seething of brilliant
expectations, but felt also that it was all a dream
which would never come true. As they intensified,
these two-edged feelings became a dark compul-
sion, a feeling as though something powerful wanted
to tear free within him and come into the open—

perhaps a sob, perhaps a song, a scream or a loud laugh. Only at home did he calm down a little. Everything there, naturally, was as usual.

"Where are you coming from?" asked Herr Giebenrath.

"From Flaig's cider mill."

"How many barrels?"

"Two, I think."

Hans asked to be allowed to invite Flaig's children when his father pressed his cider.

"Makes sense," grumbled his father. "I'll start next week, you can bring them then."

It was an hour before he would have supper. Hans went out into the garden. Except for the two spruce trees little was left that was green. He ripped off a hazel-bush rod and whipped it through the air and stirred about with it in the dried leaves. The sun had set behind the mountain whose black outline cut through the greenish-blue, moisture-free, late afternoon sky with its finely delineated spruce tops. A gray, elongated cloud, burnished by the sun, drifted slowly and contentedly like a returning ship through the thin golden air up the valley.

As Hans strolled through the garden, he felt moved in a strange and unfamiliar way by the ripe, richly colored beauty of the evening. Often he would stop, close his eyes and try to picture Emma to himself, how she had stood across from him at the press, how she let him drink from her beaker, how she had bent across the vat and come up blushing. He saw her hair, her figure in the tight blue dress, her throat and the neck in the shadow of her dark curls, and all this filled him with desire and trembling. Only her face he could not imagine, however hard he tried.

Once the sun had set he did not feel the coolness. He perceived the growing dusk like a veil rich with secret promises which he could not name. For, though he realized that he had fallen in love with the girl from Heilbronn, he had only an obscure comprehension of the masculinity awakening in his blood as an unaccustomed, wearisome irritation.

During supper he felt it was odd to sit in his changed condition amid his accustomed surroundings. His father, the old housekeeper, the table, its utensils and the entire room seemed suddenly to have grown old and he peered at everything with a feeling of astonishment, estrangement and tenderness as though he had just now returned from a long trip.

When they had finished supper and Hans wanted to get up, his father in his curt manner said: "Would you like to become a mechanic, Hans, or a clerk?"

"What do you mean?" Hans replied in astonishment.

"You could start your apprenticeship with Mechanic Schuler or week after next go to city hall. Give it some thought! We'll talk about it tomorrow."

Hans got up and went outside. The sudden question had confused and blinded him. Unexpectedly, active daily life, with which he had nothing to do for months, confronted him with a half-enticing, a half-threatening face, making promises and demands. He had no genuine enthusiasm for becoming a mechanic or a clerk. The grueling physical labor of the former frightened him a little. Then he remembered his schoolfriend August, who had become a mechanic and whom he could ask.

While he considered the matter, his ideas on the subject became less and less clear and it no longer seemed so urgent. Something else preoccupied him. Restless, he paced back and forth in the hallway. Suddenly he grabbed his hat, left the house and walked slowly out into the street. It had occurred to him he would have to see Emma once more today.

It was getting dark already. Screams and hoarse singing drifted over from a nearby inn. Some windows were lighted and here and there one after the other lit up and shed a weak reddish glow in the dark air. A long line of young girls flounced arm in arm down the alley with loud laughter and talk running like a warm wave of youth and joy through the drowsy streets. Hans looked after them for a long time, his blood rushing to his head. One could hear a violin behind a curtained window. A woman was washing lettuce at the well. Two

fellows and their sweethearts were strolling on the
bridge; one of them, holding his girl loosely by
the hand, was swinging her arm back and forth
and smoking a cigar. The second couple walked
slowly, holding each other tight; the fellow held
her firmly around the waist and she pressed
shoulder and head firmly against his chest. Hans
had seen this a hundred times without giving it
any thought. Now it held a secret significance, a
vague yet sweet and provocative meaning; his
glance rested on this group and his imagination
strained toward an imminent comprehension.
Fearful but shaken to the roots of his being, he
felt the nearness of a great mystery, not knowing
whether it would be delicious or dreadful but having a foretaste of both.

He stopped before Flaig's house but he had not
the courage to enter. What was he to do and say
once inside? He remembered how he used to come
here as an eleven-year-old boy, when Flaig had
told him stories from the Bible and steadfastly
replied to the onslaught of his questions about
hell, the devil and ghosts. These were awkward
memories and they made him feel guilty. He did
not know what he wanted to do, he did not even
know what he desired, yet it seemed to him as
though he stood before something secret and forbidden. It did not seem right to him to stand in
front of the shoemaker's house in the dark without
entering. And if Flaig should happen to see him

or should step outside he would probably not even bawl him out, he'd just laugh, and that he dreaded most of all.

Hans sneaked behind the house to look into the lighted living room from the garden fence. He did not see the master anywhere. His wife was either sewing or knitting. The oldest boy was still up and sat at the table and read. Emma walked back and forth, obviously clearing the table, and he caught sight of her only intermittently. It was so quiet you could hear every step distinctly from the remotest part of the street, and the rushing of the river on the other side of the garden. The darkness and the chill of night came fast.

Next to the living-room window was a small unlit hall window. After he had waited for some time there appeared at this window an indistinct shape, which leaned out and looked into the darkness. Hans recognized from the shape that it was Emma and his heart palpitated with apprehension. She stood at the window for a long while, calmly looking across to him, yet he had no idea whether she recognized him or even saw him. He did not move once and just peered in her direction, wavering between hope and fear that she might see who it was.

And the shape vanished from the window. Immediately afterward the little bell at the garden door chimed and Emma came out of the house. At first Hans was so scared he wanted to run off, but then he stayed, leaning against the fence, unable to move, and watched the girl approach him slowly in the dark garden. With each step she took, he felt the urge to run off but something stronger held him back.

Now Emma stood directly in front of him, no more than half a step away, and with only the fence between, she peered at him attentively and curiously. For a long time neither of them said a word. Then she asked:

"What do you want, Hans?"

"Nothing," he replied and it was as if she had caressed him when she called him Hans.

She stretched her hand across the fence. He held it timidly and tenderly and pressed it a little. When he realized that it was not being withdrawn, he took heart and stroked the warm hand. And when it was still left to him to hold, he placed it against his cheek. A flood of desire, peculiar warmth and blissful weariness coursed through him. The air seemed lukewarm and moist. The street and garden became invisible. All he saw was a close bright face and a tangle of dark hair.

Her voice seemed to reach him from far-off in the night when she said very softly:

"Do you want to kiss me?"

The bright face came closer, the weight of the body bent the fence boards slightly toward him; loose, lightly scented hair brushed his forehead, and closed eyes with wide lids and dark eyelashes were near to his. A strong shudder ran through his body as he shyly placed his lips on the girl's mouth. He shied back trembling at once but the girl had seized his head, pressed her face to his and would not let go of his lips. He felt her mouth burn, he felt it press against his and cling to him as if she wanted to drain all life from him. A profound weakness overcame him; even before her lips let go of him, his trembling desire changed into deathly weariness and pain, and when Emma unloosed him, he felt unsteady and had to clutch the fence for support.

"You come back tomorrow evening," said Emma and quickly slipped back into the house. She had not been with him for more than five minutes but it seemed to Hans as if hours had passed. He gazed after her with an empty stare, still holding onto the fence, and felt too tired to take a single step. As if in a dream he listened to his blood pounding through his brain in irregular, painful surges, coming from the heart and rushing back, making him gasp for breath.

Now, through the window, he saw a door open inside the living room and the master enter; probably he had been in his workshop. Suddenly Hans became afraid he might be seen and he left. He walked slowly, reluctantly, with the uncertainty of someone who is slightly intoxicated. With each step he felt like going down on his knees. The dark streets, the drowsy gables, the dimly lit red windows flowed past like a pale stage setting. The

fountain in Tanner Street splashed with unusual
resonance. As if in a dream he opened a gate,
walked through a pitch-black hallway, climbed a
series of stairs, opened and closed one door after
another, sat down at a table that happened to be
there and only after some time did he become
aware of being home in his room. There was another
long pause before he could decide to undress. He
did it distractedly and sat undressed in the window
for a long time until the fall night suddenly chilled
him and drove him between the sheets.

He felt he would fall asleep that instant but he
had no sooner lain down than his heart began to
throb again and there was the irregular violent
surging of his blood. When he closed his eyes, it
seemed as if Emma's lips were still clinging to his,
draining his soul, filling him with fever.

It was late at night before he fell into a sleep
which hurried in a headlong flight from dream
to dream. He was steeped in darkness, and groping
about, he seized Emma's arm. She embraced him
and they slowly sank down together into a deep
warm flood. Suddenly the shoemaker was there and
asked him why he refused to visit him; then Hans
had to laugh when he noticed that it was not
Flaig but Heilner who sat next to him in the alcove in the Maulbronn oratory, cracking jokes.
But this image also vanished at once and he saw
himself standing by the cider press, Emma pushing
against the lever and he struggling against her
with all his might. She bent across the vat feeling

for his mouth. It became quiet and pitch-black. Now he once more sank into that deep warm depth and seemed to die with dizziness. Simultaneously he could hear the headmaster deliver a lecture but he could not tell whether it was meant for him.

He slept until late in the morning. It was a bright, sunny day. He walked up and down in the garden for a long time, trying to become fully awake and clear his mind which seemed enveloped by a thick drowsy fog. He could see violet asters, the very last flowers to bloom, standing in the sunshine as though it were still August, and he saw the dear warm light flood tenderly and insinuatingly around the withered bushes, branches and leafless vines as though it were early spring. But he only saw it, he did not experience it, it did not matter to him. Suddenly he was seized by a recollection of the time when his rabbits were still scurrying about the garden and his water wheel and his little mill were running. He thought back to a particular day in September, three years ago. It was the evening before the day commemorating the battle of Sedan. August had come over to see him and had brought some ivy vines along. They washed down their flagpoles until they glistened and then fastened the ivy to the golden spikes, looking forward with eagerness to the coming day. Not much else happened but both of them were so full of anticipation and joy. Anna had baked

plum cakes and that night the Sedan fire was to
be lit on the rock on the mountain.

Hans could think of no reason why that evening came back to him now, nor why its memory
was so overpoweringly beautiful, nor why it made
him feel so miserably sad. He did not realize that
his childhood took on this shape and dress once
more before departing from him, leaving only the
sting of a happiness that would never return. All
he perceived was that these memories did not fit
in with his thoughts of Emma and of the previous evening and that something had happened
that could not be combined with his childhood
happiness. He thought he could see the golden
spikes on the flags glisten once more in the sunlight and hear his friend August laugh, and all
of that seemed so glad and cheerful in retrospect
that he leaned against the rough bark of the great
spruce and broke into a fit of hopeless sobbing
which brought him momentary relief and consolation.

Around noon he went to look up August, who
had just been made senior apprentice. He had
filled out considerably and grown much taller since
Hans saw him last. Hans told him of his father's
suggestion.

"That's a problem," was August's first response.
He put on an experienced, worldly-wise expression. "That's a problem, all right . . . because
you're not what I would call a muscle-man. The

first day you'll be standing at the smithy all day long swinging the forge-hammer, and a hammer like that is no soup ladle. You'll be lugging the heavy iron around all day, you'll clean up in the evening, and handling a file isn't child's play either, you'll only get the oldest and worst files to use until you know the ropes, files that don't cut anything and are as smooth as a baby's ass."

Hans' confidence dropped instantly.

"Well, do you think I should forget the idea?" he asked timidly.

"Ho there! That's not what I said. Don't drop your pants. I just meant that at the beginning it's no child's play. But otherwise, well, being a mechanic can be pretty good, you know. And you've got to have a head on your shoulders, or you'll just be a blacksmith. Here, have a look."

He took out a few small finely worked machine parts made of glistening steel and showed them to Hans.

"Yes, you can't be off a half-millimeter with these. All made by hand except for the screws. It means eyes open and a steady hand! All they need is some polishing and tempering; then they're ready."

"Yes, that's beautiful. If I just knew . . ."

August laughed.

"You afraid? Well, an apprentice is chewed out lots of the time. No two ways about that. But I'll be here and I'll help you and if you start next Friday I'll just have finished my second year and'll get my first wages on Saturday and on Sunday we'll celebrate with beer and a cake and everything. You too, then, you'll see for yourself what it's like here. And besides, we used to be friends before."

At lunch Hans informed his father he'd like to become a mechanic and asked whether he could start working in a week.

"Well, fine," said Giebenrath senior, and in the afternoon he took Hans to Schuler's workshop and signed him up.

By the time dusk set in, Hans had almost forgotten his new job. All he could think of was meeting Emma in the evening. This took his breath away. The hours passed too slowly, then too quickly; he drifted into the encounter like a boatman into rapids. All he had for supper was a glass of milk. Then he left.

It was just like the night before: dark, drowsy streets, dimly lit windows, lanterns' twilight, couples ambling.

At the shoemaker's garden fence he became apprehensive, flinched at every noise. Standing there he felt like a thief listening in the dark. He had not waited more than a minute when Emma stood before him, stroked his hair, then opened the gate for him to come into the garden. He entered carefully. She drew him after her quietly along the path bordered by bushes, through the back door into the dark hallway.

There they sat down on the topmost step of the

cellar stairs. It was a while before they could make each other out in the dark. The girl was in high spirits, chattering and whispering. She had been kissed before, she knew something about love; this shy, affectionate boy was just right for her. She took his head in her hands and kissed his eyes, cheeks, and when it was the mouth's turn she again kissed him so long and so fervently that the boy leaned dizzy, limp, without a will of his own against her. She laughed softly and pinched his ear.

She chatted on and on. He listened not knowing what it was he heard. She stroked his arm, his hair, his neck and his hands, she leaned her cheek against his and her head on his shoulder. He kept silent and let everything happen, filled as he was with a sweet dread and a profound and happy fearfulness, only flinching occasionally, softly, briefly, like someone in a fever.

"What a boyfriend you are!" she laughed. "You don't try anything at all."

And she took his hand and stroked her neck with it, passed it through her hair and laid it against her breast, pressing against it. He felt the soft bosom and the unfamiliar heaving, closed his eyes and felt himself swooning into infinite depths.

"No! No more!" he said fending her off as she tried to kiss him anew. She laughed.

And she drew him to her and hugged him so tight that, feeling her body against his, he went out of his mind.

"Don't you love me?" she asked.

He could not say a thing. He wanted to say yes but could only nod—so he just kept nodding for a while.

Once more she took his hand and with a laugh placed it under her bodice. When he felt the pulse and breath of another life so hot and close to him, his heart stopped, he was sure he was dying, he was breathing so heavily. He drew back his hand and groaned: "I've got to go home now."

When he tried to get up he began to totter and nearly fell down the cellar stairs.

"What's the matter?" asked Emma, astonished.

"I don't know. I feel so tired."

He did not notice how she propped him up on the way to the garden gate, pressing against him, nor when she said good night and closed the gate behind him. Somehow he found his way home through the streets, he did not know how, as though a great storm dragged him along or as though a mighty flood tossed him back and forth.

He saw pale houses, mountain ridges above them, spruce tops, night blackness and big calm stars. He felt the wind blow, heard the river stream past the bridge posts, saw the gardens, pale houses, night blackness, lanterns and stars reflected in the water.

On the bridge he had to sit down. He felt so tired he didn't believe he'd make it home. He sat down on the railing, listened to the water rubbing against the pilings, roaring over the weirs, cascading down the milldam. His hands were cold, his chest and throat worked fitfully, blood shot into his brain and flooded back to his heart leaving his head dizzy. He came home, found his room, lay down and fell asleep at once, tumbling from one depth to the next in his dreams—through immense spaces. Around midnight he awoke, exhausted and in pain. He lay half-waking, half-sleeping until early dawn, filled with an unquenchable longing, tossed hither and thither by uncontrollable forces until his whole agony and oppression exploded into a prolonged fit of weeping. He fell asleep once more on tear-soaked pillows.

Chapter Seven

HERR GIEBENRATH applied himself to his work at the cider press with dignity and considerable noise; Hans helped him. Two of Flaig's children had responded to the invitation. They were sorting apples, shared a little glass between them with which they sampled cider, and clutched big hunks of bread in their fists. But Emma had not come with them.

Not until his father had been gone for half an hour with the cooper did Hans dare ask where she was.

"Where's Emma? Didn't she feel like coming?"

It took a few moments for the children to swallow and clear their throats.

"She's gone, she has," they said and nodded.

"Gone? Gone where?"

"Home."

"With the train?"

The children nodded eagerly.

"When?"

"This morning."

The children again reached for their apples.

Hans fumbled about at the press, stared into the cider keg until the truth slowly dawned on him.

When his father came back, they worked and laughed, and finally the children said thank you and ran off. At dusk, everyone went home.

After supper Hans sat alone in his room. It turned ten, then eleven o'clock, and he did not light his lamp. Then he fell into a long deep sleep.

At first, when he awoke later than usual, he had only an indistinct feeling of an accident or loss. Then he remembered Emma. She had left without saying good-bye, without leaving a message. She must have known when she would be leaving the last night he'd seen her. He remembered her laughter and her kisses and the accomplished way she had of surrendering herself. She hadn't taken him seriously at all.

The pain and anger over this loss and the restlessness of his inflamed but unsatisfied passion came together in a single agonizing confusion. The torment drove him from the house into the garden, then onto the streets and into the woods and finally back home again.

In this way he discovered—perhaps too soon— his share of the secret of love, and it contained little sweetness and much bitterness: days filled with fruitless lamentation, poignant memories, inconsolable brooding; nights during which a pounding heart and tightness around the chest would not let him sleep or plagued him with dreadful nightmares; nightmares during which the incomprehensible agitation of his blood turned into haunting images, into deathly, strangling arms, into hot-eyed fantastic ogres, dizzying precipices, giant flaming eyes. Waking, he found himself alone in his room, surrounded by the loneliness of a cool fall night. Hans suffered with longing for his girl and tried to suppress his moans in a tear-stained pillow.

The Friday when he was to begin his appenticeship drew near. His father bought him a set of blue overalls and a blue woolen cap. Hans tried the outfit on and felt quite ridiculous in it. Whenever he passed the school house, the principal's house or the math teacher's, Flaig's workshop or the vicarage, he felt quite wretched. So much effort, so much pride and ambition and hope and dreaming —and all for nothing. All of it only so that now, later than any of his former schoolmates and ridiculed by all, he could become the junior apprentice in a mechanic's workshop.

What would Heilner have said?

It took some time for him to reconcile himself to his blue mechanic's outfit but finally he began looking forward a little to the Friday on which he would be initiated. At least he would be experiencing something again!

Yet these hopes were not much more than glimmers in a generally gloomy sky. He could not forget the girl's departure, and his blood seemed even less willing to forget the agitation of those days. It gave him no peace and clamored for more, for relief from the awakened desire. And so time passed with oppressive slowness.

Fall was more beautiful than ever—with a gentle sun, silvery mornings, colorful bright middays, clear evenings. The more distant mountains assumed a deep velvety blue, the chestnut trees shone golden yellow and the wild grapevine curtained walls and fences purple.

Hans was in a state of restless flight from himself. In the daytime he roamed through town and fields. He avoided people since he felt they could detect his lovelorn state. But in the evening he went out into the streets, made eyes at every maid and crept guiltily after every pair of lovers. The magic of life and everything he had ever sought seemed to have been within reach with Emma. But even with her it had eluded his grasp. If she were with him now, so he believed, he would not be timid; no, he would tear every secret from her and completely penetrate that garden of love whose gate had been slammed in his face. His imagination had become inextricably tangled in this murky and dangerous thicket: straying despondently, his imagination preferred stubborn self-torment to acknowledging the existence of clear friendly spaces outside this confining, magic circle.

In the end he was glad when the dreaded Friday arrived. With no time to spare in the morning, he donned his new blue outfit and cap and walked down Tanner Street, a little timidly, toward Schuler's workshop. A few acquaintances looked at him inquisitively and one even asked: "What's happened, you becoming a locksmith?"

The shop already resounded with the din of work. The master himself was busy forging. He had a piece of red-hot iron on the anvil and one of the journeymen was wielding the heavy sledge hammer, the master himself only executing the finer, form-giving blows, handling the tongs which held the iron, and striking so rhythmically with the lighter forge hammer that it rang out through the wide-open door clear and bright into the morning.

The senior journeyman and August both stood at the long workbench black with grease and iron filings, each of them busy at his vise. Along the ceiling purred the rapidly moving belts that drove the lathes, grindstone, bellows and drilling machine—all driven by water power. August nodded to his companion as he entered and motioned to him to wait at the door until the master had time for him.

Hans gazed timidly at the forge, lathes, the whirring belts and the neutral gears. When the master had finished forging his piece of iron he came over and extended his warm, callused hand. "You hang your cap up there," he said and pointed to an empty nail on the wall. "Now come with me. There's your place and your vise." With that he led Hans to the vise farthest in the back. He demonstrated how a vise is handled and how you keep your bench and tools in order.

"Your father already told me that you're no Hercules, and I guess he's right. Well, until you're a little stronger you don't have to work at the forge."

He reached under the workbench and drew out a cast-iron cogwheel.

"You can start on that. The wheel is still rough from the casting and has little knobs and ridges all over. They've got to be filed off, otherwise the fine tools will be ruined later on."

He clamped the wheel into the vise, picked up an old file and showed Hans how it was done.

"Well, now you take it from here. But don't you use any other of my files! That'll keep you busy till lunch break. Then you can show it to me. And while you're working don't pay attention to anything but your instructions. An apprentice doesn't need to have ideas of his own."

Hans started to file.

"Stop!" shouted the master. "Not like that. You put your left hand on top of the file. Or are you a lefty?"

"No."

"Well, all right. It'll work out somehow."

He went back to his vise, the one nearest the door, and Hans tried to do his best.

As he made his first strokes he was surprised how soft the ridges were and how easily they came off. Then he realized that only the topmost brittle coating was flaking off and the granular iron he had to file off was underneath. He pulled himself together and kept on filing. Not since the days of his boyhood hobbies had he tasted the pleasure of seeing something concrete and useful take shape under his hands.

"Not so fast!" shouted the master over the din. "You've got to file in rhythm: one-two, one-two, and press on it, or you'll ruin the file."

The oldest of the journeymen had to go to the lathe, and Hans could not keep from glancing in his direction. A drill bit was fitted into the chuck, the belt was moved into position, and the shining drill buzzed while the journeyman severed a hair-thin glinting steel shaving from it.

All around lay tools, pieces of iron, steel and brass, half-completed jobs, shining little wheels, chisels, drills, drill bits and awls of every shape and size; next to the forge hung the hammers, top and bottom tools, anvil, tongs and soldering irons. Along the walls lay rows of files and cutting files; along the shelves lay oil rags, little brooms, emery files, iron saws and oil cans, soldering fluid, boxes with nails and screws. Every moment someone or other had to go to the grindstone.

Hans noted with satisfaction that his hands were already black and hoped that his overalls would follow suit, for they still looked ridiculously new and blue next to the black and patched outfits of the others.

Later on in the morning people coming from the outside brought even more activity into the shop. Workers came from the nearby garment factory to have small parts ground or repaired. A farmer came and asked about a mangle of his they were repairing and cursed blasphemously when it was not ready. Then a smartly dressed factory owner came and the master took him to a room off to the side.

In the midst of all this, people, wheels and belts went on working smoothly, evenly, and thus for the first time in his life Hans understood labor's song of songs—work. It has—at least for the beginner—something enchanting and pleasantly intoxicating as he beholds his own small person and own small life become a part of a greater rhythm.

At nine o'clock they had a fifteen-minute break and everyone received a chunk of bread and glass of cider. Only now could August greet the new apprentice. He talked to him encouragingly and enthused some more about the upcoming Sunday on which he wanted to treat his friends to a great spree with his first wages. Hans asked him what kind of wheel that was which he was filing smooth and was told that it was part of the watchworks of a tower clock. August was about to demonstrate the part it would play in the mechanism when the senior journeyman picked up his file again and they all quickly went back to their places.

Between ten and eleven Hans felt himself tiring. His knees and his right arm ached a little. He kept shifting his weight from one leg to the other and surreptitiously stretched his limbs, but it did not help much. So he put down the file for a moment and rested against the vise. No one was paying any attention to him. As he stood there resting and heard the belts whirring above him, he felt slightly dizzy and he closed his eyes for a minute. Just then the master came up behind him.

"Well, what is it? Pooped already?"

"A bit," Hans admitted.

The journeyman laughed.

"You'll get over that," the master said calmly. "Now you come along and see how we solder."

Hans watched with fascination. First the soldering iron was heated, then the spot to be soldered was covered with chlorate of zinc, then the white metal dripped from the iron, gently hissing.

"Now you take a rag and wipe the spot clean. Soldering fluid corrodes, so you can't leave any on metal."

Hans went back to his vise and scratched away at his wheel. His arm hurt and his left hand with which he pressed down on the file had become red and began to smart.

Around noon when the senior journeyman put away his file and went to wash his hands, Hans took his work to the master, who gave it a cursory inspection.

"That's all right, you can leave it like that. Under your bench in the box is another just like it. You can do that this afternoon."

Now Hans washed his hands too and went home. He had an hour for lunch.

Two fellows who clerked for a businessman and with whom he had gone to grammar school followed him in the street and jeered.

"Academy mechanic!" one of them shouted.

He quickened his pace. He wasn't sure whether he was really satisfied or not. He had liked the workshop itself, only he had become so tired, so miserably tired.

As he was about to enter the house and was looking forward to the meal, he found himself thinking of Emma. He had not thought of her once all morning. He went softly into his little room, threw himself on his bed and moaned with misery. He wanted to cry but no tears would come. Again he saw himself hopelessly at the mercy of his longing. His head hurt and was in an uproar; his throat too hurt with suppressed sobs.

Lunch was sheer agony. He had to answer his father's assorted questions and tell him about the work. He endured a series of wisecracks—his father was in a jolly mood. With the meal over, he dashed into the garden and spent fifteen minutes day-dreaming in the sun. Then it was time to head back for the workshop.

By the end of the morning he had already developed red swellings on his hands and now they began to hurt seriously. By evening they had swollen so he could not hold anything without hurting. And before he could go home he had to clean up the whole workshop under August's direction.

Saturday was even worse. His hands burned, the swellings had turned into blisters, the master was in a rotten humor and flew off the handle at the least provocation. August tried to console him and said the swellings would go away in a few days, he would grow calluses and no longer feel anything. Yet Hans felt more wretched than ever, glanced at the clock throughout the day and kept scratching hopelessly at his wheel.

While cleaning up that evening August communicated to him in whispers that he and a couple of friends were going to Bielach the next day and that they intended to have a great old time and Hans would have to show, or else. Hans was to meet him at his place at two o'clock. Hans said yes but he would have preferred to spend all day Sunday in bed, he was so tired and miserable. At home Anna gave him some salve for his hands. He turned in at eight o'clock and slept until well into the morning. He had to rush not to miss church with his father.

During lunch he broached the subject of August and their going to Bielach for the afternoon. His father raised no objections, even gave him fifty pfennig, and only demanded he be back for supper.

As Hans ambled through the streets in the sunshine he realized for the first time in months with pleasure that it was Sunday. The streets were more solemn, the sun more cheerful, everything was more festive when you could leave the workday and its black hands behind. Now he understood the butchers and bakers, tanners and blacksmiths who sat on benches in front of their houses sunning themselves and looked so princely and glad; he no longer looked down on them as miserable Philistines. He watched the workers, the journeymen and apprentices, as they went in groups on Sunday walks or stopped into inns, their hats slightly tilted, with white collars and their well-brushed Sunday best. Mostly, if not always, the various members of a craft kept to themselves: carpenters with carpenters, masons with masons. They stuck together and preserved the honor of their guild, and of all of the guilds the locksmiths were the most respected, with the mechanics at the very top. All of this had something very cozy about it and even if it also contained a slightly naïve and ridiculous element, there was the traditional beauty and pride of being an artisan, a tradition which even today represents something joyful and sound and which enhances even the lowliest little apprentice.

The way the young mechanics stood in front of Schuler's house, so calm and proud, nodding to passers-by and talking among themselves, you could easily discern that they were a self-sufficient group, had no need of company, not even on Sundays when they had their fun.

This was exactly what Hans felt and he was glad to be one of them. Still, he was a little apprehensive about the planned expedition. He was well aware that the mechanics were in the habit of taking their pleasures in rather massive doses. Perhaps they would even go dancing. Hans had no idea how, but he decided to be a man even at the risk of a small hangover. He was not used to drinking quantities of beer and in the matter of smoking he had only just reached the stage where he could finish a cigar without running the danger of discomfort or disgrace.

August greeted him with easy cheerfulness. He said the senior journeyman did not want to come along but a colleague from another shop would come instead so there would be at least four of them, enough to turn a whole village upside down. Everyone could drink all the beer he wanted today, since he was paying. He offered Hans a cigar, then the four slowly got underway, ambled leisurely and proudly through town, only quickening their pace at the Lindenplatz to get to Bielach in good time.

The river reflected blue, gold and white. Through the almost bare maples and acacias you could feel the mild October sun. The sky was deep and of a cloudless light blue. It was one of those pure and tranquil friendly fall days on which everything that was beautiful in the previous summer fills the mild air with untroubled, smiling memories, when children forget what season it is and think they should be picking flowers, when old people gaze pensively from their windows, or up from benches in front of their houses into the sky because it seems to them the friendly memories of that year and of their whole long life winged visibly through the transparent blue. The young people were in high spirits and praised the day according to their gifts and temperament—by drinking or slaughtering an animal, by singing or dancing, by drinking bouts or suffering. Everywhere fruitcakes and pies were being baked, young cider and wine were fermenting in the cellars, and fiddles and accordions in front of inns and under the linden in the squares celebrated the last beautiful days of the year, inviting the world to dance and sing and make love.

The young fellows were making rapid headway. Hans smoked his cigar with a semblance of carelessness and was himself surprised how well it became him. The journeyman recounted his years spent traveling about and no one objected to his boasting. That was part of the act. Even the most unassuming little apprentice, once he gets into the thick of his subject and is among his own kind and safe from eyewitnesses, will coolly lace his account of his traveling days with legendary attributes. For the marvelous poetry of the life the artisans and apprentices lead is the common property of the people. The traditional adventures are reincarnated in every one of them and adorned with new variations, and every journeyman, once he really gets going, is a bit of the eternal Eulenspiegel and the undying Straubinger.

"Man, the last time in Frankfurt, what a wild

town that was! Didn't I tell you how a rich guy, a big business man, wanted to marry the boss's daughter but she gave him the sack because she liked me better? She was my girl for four months and if I hadn't gotten in a fix with the old man I'd still be there and his son-in-law."

And he went on to tell how his master, the bastard, had tried to give him a hard time, the miserable s.o.b., and once he even dared raise his hand against him but he didn't say a word, he just kept swinging that sledge hammer and gave the old man a look and the old man just sort of slunk away because he didn't want to have his head bashed in and then he gave him notice, the drip, in writing. And he went on to tell about a big street fight in Offenburg, where three locksmiths, he among them, had tangled with seven factory guys and knocked them half dead—anyone coming to Offenburg, all he had to do was ask that beanstalk Schorsch, who's still there and who was along back then.

All of this was communicated in a cool, tough voice, but with great intensity and delight, and everyone listened with pleasure and made up his mind to tell that story someday somewhere else with other companions. For every locksmith has had his master's daughter for a sweetheart at one time or other and has taken off after the evil master with a hammer and beaten the daylights out of seven factory workers. One time the story is set in Baden, next in Hessen or Switzerland; once it is a file or a slug of red-hot iron and not a hammer; sometimes the victims are not factory workers but bakers or tailors but the stories are invariably the same, and you like hearing them again and again because they are old and good and bring honor to the craft. None of which is meant to imply that the traveling artisans lack fellows in their midst— even today—who are not geniuses in experiencing or inventing, which are basically one and the same thing.

August in particular was delighted and completely swept off his feet. He laughed continuously and said yes, yes, yes, already considered himself a journeyman for all intents and purposes and blew tobacco smoke with epicurean disdain into the golden air. And the narrator continued to enjoy his role, for it mattered to him that his coming along would appear as a good-natured act of condescension since as a journeyman he, properly speaking, did not belong in the company of apprentices on a sunday and should have been ashamed of himself for helping an apprentice drink up his first earnings.

They had walked a good ways down along the river and now had a choice between taking the gradually rising dirt road which curves lazily up the mountain or the steep footpath which was only half as long. They decided on the dirt road, though it was longer and dustier. Footpaths are for working days and for gentlemen on walks; but the common people prefer the regular country roads, especially on Sundays—these roads have retained their poetry for the people. To climb steep footpaths is something for farmers, or for nature lovers from the city; that is either work or a sport but not a pleasure. On a country road, however, you can make leisurely headway and can talk and don't wear out your soles or clothes, see carts and horses, meet other people just as leisurely as yourself, overtake girls all dressed up and groups of singing fellows. People will call out jokes to you and you will laugh and parry them; you can stop and chat, and if you have nothing better to do, run after girls and laugh after them, and in the evening you can settle personal differences with your companions by taking direct action.

Thus they took the country road. The journeyman took off his coat, hung it on his stick and then shouldered the stick; instead of telling stories he had begun to whistle in an altogether daring and vivacious manner and he did not stop whistling until they reached Bielach an hour later. Hans had been the victim of a little needling but it had not penetrated very deep and these attacks were parried more eagerly by August than by himself. And now they stood at the edge of Bielach.

The village with its red-tile and silver-gray thatched roofs lay couched among autumn-tinted orchards, a dark densely forested mountain rising up in back.

They could not agree which tavern they should enter. The Anchor served the best beer but the

Swan the best cake and Sharp Corner possessed a pretty innkeeper's daughter. Finally August's suggestion prevailed that they should first head for the Anchor, adding with a wink that the Sharp Corner probably would not run off while they had a few steins. No one had any objection to this so they entered the village, walked past animal pens, low farmhouse windows decked with geraniums and headed for the Anchor whose golden sign gleamed invitingly in the sun above two young chestnut trees. To the chagrin of the journeyman, who insisted on sitting inside, the bar was overcrowded already and they had to sit outside in the garden.

Its guests regarded the Anchor as a first-rate tavern, not, in other words, some old farmer's inn but a modern brick building with far too many windows, with chairs instead of wooden benches and a clutter of metal advertising signs, as well as a waitress in city clothes and an innkeeper whom you never caught with his sleeves rolled up but who always wore a modish brown suit. Actually he was bankrupt but he had mortgaged his house to his main creditor, the owner of a big brewery, and since then assumed an even more dignified air. The garden consisted of an acacia tree and a big wire fence, for the time being half overgrown with wild grapevines.

"To your health," shouted the journeyman and clinked steins with the three others. And to prove his mettle he chuggalugged the whole mug.

"Hey, miss, there wasn't anything in that one. Bring me another," he called after the waitress and handed her the mug across the table.

The beer was excellent, cool, and not too dry. Hans enjoyed it thoroughly. August drank with the air of a connoisseur, simultaneously clicked his tongue and smoked like an oven in ill repair—something which Hans quietly admired.

It was not so bad after all then to go on a Sunday spree and sit at such a table like someone who has the right to, and with people who got a kick out of life. It felt good to join in the laughter and venture an occasional joke of your own; it was good and manly to slam your mug on the table when you were finished and call out without a care in the world: "Hey, miss, another!" It was good to drink a toast to an acquaintance at a nearby table, the butt of your cigar dangling from your left hand, your hat pushed back onto your head, like everyone else's hat.

The colleague from the other shop began to unthaw too and to tell stories of his own. He told about a locksmith in Ulm who drank twenty mugs of beer at a sitting, and of the good Ulm beer, and when it was finished he would wipe his mouth once and say: "Now let's have a bottle of wine for a chaser!" And he had known a stoker in Cannstatt who could eat twelve knockwursts in a row and had won a bet that way. But he had lost a second bet just like it. He had bet he could eat everything on the menu of a small inn and he'd eaten his way down to the cheeses and when he reached his third cheese he just pushed the platter away and said: "I'd rather die than eat another bite."

These stories too were well received. It became clear to Hans that on this earth there must exist a goodly number of endurance drinkers and eaters, for everyone knows about one such hero and his feats. One can tell about a man in Stuttgart, another about a dragoon, I think in Ludwigsburg, one story has seventeen potatoes, another eleven pancakes and a salad. All these events are recounted with professional seriousness and everyone takes comfort in the realization that—after all —there exist all sorts of remarkable people and beautiful talents, and crazy fools. This sense of well-being is an old and honorable heirloom of tavern conventions and it's imitated by the young just as they imitate drinking, talking politics, smoking, marrying and dying.

While they were at their third mug, one of them asked for some cake. The waitress was hailed and they were told there was no cake. They all became quite wrought up. August rose to his feet and announced that if this place didn't even have cake, they might as well hit the next inn down the street. The colleague cursed about what a lousy way it was to run a business; only the journeyman wanted to stay—he had been flirting with the waitress, had even stroked her bottom in passing. Hans had noticed and this sight plus the ef-

fect of the beer had excited him strangely. He
was glad they moved on.

Once the bill was paid and all of them stepped
out on the street, Hans began to feel slightly
affected by his three mugs of beer. It was a pleasant sensation, half weariness, half devil-may-care.
He was conscious too of something like a thin veil
before his eyes through which everything looked
more remote, almost unreal and much as it looks
in dreams. He could not help giggling, had set his
hat at an even more rakish angle and considered
himself one hell of a fellow. The Frankfurt journeyman whistled again in his tough way and Hans
tried to keep the beat.

It was pretty quiet in the Sharp Corner. A
couple of farmers were sampling the new wine.
There was no draft beer, only bottles, and each of
them was immediately served one. The colleague
journeyman wanted to prove how grand he was and
ordered an apple pie big enough for all of them.
Hans suddenly felt hunger pangs and ate several
slices in quick succession. It was comfortably dark
on the firm, wide benches along the wall in the
old dark-brown barroom. The old-fashioned counter
and the huge stove were no longer distinguishable
in the semi-darkness; in a big cage built of wooden
staves fluttered two songbirds. A whole branch
with red birdberries had been thrust through the
staves for them.

The host stopped at their table for a moment
and bade them welcome. After that it took a while

for a real conversation to develop. Hans took a few gulps from the tart bottled beer and wondered whether he was going to be able to down the whole bottle.

The journeyman was carrying on again about wine festivals in the Rhineland, his journeyman days and what a vagabond life he had led. They all listened in high spirits and even Hans could not stop laughing.

Suddenly he became aware that something was not quite right with him. Every few seconds or so the room, the tables, bottles and glasses and his companions merged into a brownish miasma, and only by a great effort on his part did they regain their outlines. From time to time, when the conversations and laughter rose in volume, he would join the laughter, add a comment and forget immediately what he'd said. When they clinked glasses he joined in and after some time he realized that his quart was empty.

"That's quite an intake you have," said August. "Want another?"

Hans nodded and laughed. He'd always thought that such a drinking bout would be much more dangerous. And now the journeyman intoned a song and they all joined in and Hans sang with as much fervor as the rest.

Meanwhile the room had filled up and the inn-keeper's daughter came to lend the waitress a hand. She was a tall, well-built girl with a healthy, vigorous face and calm brown eyes.

When she placed the new bottle in front of Hans, the journeyman who was sitting next to him instantly showered her with elegant compliments, but she paid him no mind. Perhaps because she wanted to show him her indifference or perhaps because she had taken a liking to the boy's finely shaped face, she turned to Hans and quickly ran her hand through his hair; then she went back behind the counter.

The Journeyman, who was on his third bottle, followed her and went to great lengths to engage her in conversation but without success. The big girl looked at him evenly, made no reply and turned her back on him. Then he came back, drummed his empty bottle on the table and called out with sudden enthusiasm: "Come, fellows, let's be happy, clink glasses."

And then he launched into a good dirty story.

All that Hans could make out at this point was a murky hubbub of voices, and when he had almost finished his second bottle, he found he had difficulty speaking and even laughing. He felt the urge to go over to the cage and tease the birds but after several steps he became dizzy, nearly fell down and carefully retraced his steps.

From that point on his mood of abandon and gaiety began to wane. When he knew he was drunk the whole business of drinking lost its appeal. And as if at a great distance he saw all sorts of misfortunes awaiting him: the way home, trouble with his father and next morning back at the shop. Gradually his head began to ache.

The others had had their fill too. In a lucid moment August decided to pay up and received only meager change for his bill. Gabbing and laughing loudly, they emerged into the street, blinded by the bright evening light. Hans was barely able to walk upright; he leaned unsteadily against August who dragged him along.

The colleague had now become sentimental. He was singing: "Tomorrow I must leave this place," with tears in his eyes.

Actually they wanted to head home but when they passed the Swan the journeyman insisted on stopping by briefly. Hans tore free at the entrance.

"I've got to go home," he uttered.

"But you can hardly walk straight by yourself," laughed the journeyman.

"I can. I can. I—must—go—home."

"Well, at least have one schnapps with us. That'll put you back on your feet and settle your stomach. You'll see."

Hans felt a glass in his hand. He spilled a good deal of it and the rest coursed down his gullet like a firebrand. He was shaken by a strong feeling of nausea. Alone he stumbled down the front steps and came—he hardly knew how—out of the village. Houses, fences, gardens wheeled crookedly and confusedly past him. He lay down in a wet meadow under an apple tree. Hideous sensations, agonizing fears and half-finished thoughts kept him from falling asleep. He felt filthy and defiled. How was he to get home? What was he to say to his father? And what was to become of him tomorrow? He felt shattered and wretched as though he would have to rest and sleep and be ashamed of himself for the rest of his life. His head and eyes ached and he did not even feel strong enough to get up and go on.

Suddenly a touch of his former gaiety returned fleetingly; he made a grimace and sang:

> "O du lieber Augustin,
> Augustin, Augustin,
> O du lieber Augustin,
> Alles ist hin."

And he had barely finished singing when something in his innermost being flashed with pain, and a murky flood of unclear images and memories, of shame and self-reproach rushed at him. He groaned loudly and sank sobbing into the grass.

An hour later when it was getting dark he got up and walked unsteadily and with great effort down the hill.

Herr Giebenrath delivered a set of loud curses when his boy did not appear for supper. When nine o'clock struck and he still hadn't come he took out the cane. The fellow seemed to think he'd outgrown his father's rod, did he? Well, he had a little surprise waiting for him at home!

At ten he locked the front door. If his son wanted to carouse all night, he could find himself another bed to sleep in.

Still, he himself could not fall asleep but waited hour after hour with growing anger for Hans to try the door and then timidly pull the bell. He could picture the scene—that night owl had it coming to him. He'd probably be drunk but he'd sober up fast, the louse, the dirty little sneak. And if he had to break every bone in his body ...

Finally sleep overcame him and his fury.

At this very instant the boy who was the object of all these threats was drifting slowly down the cool river. All nausea, shame and suffering had passed from him; the cold bluish autumn night looked down on the dark shape of his drifting body and the dark water played with his hands and hair and bloodless lips. No one saw him floating downstream, except perhaps an otter setting out even before daybreak for the hunt, eying him cagily as he glided past without a sound. No one knew how he came to be in the water. Perhaps he had lost his way and slipped at some steep spot by the river bank; perhaps he had been thirsty and had lost his balance; perhaps the sight of the beautiful water had attracted him and when he bent over the water the night and the pale moon had seemed so peaceful and restful that weariness and fear drove him with quiet inevitability into the shadow of death.

His body was found sometime during the day and was carried home. The startled father had to put aside his cane and relinquish his pent-up fury. Although he did not weep and made little show of his feelings, he remained awake all that night and occasionally he glanced through a crack in the door at his silent child stretched out on clean sheets: the delicate forehead and pale, intelligent face still made him look like someone special, whose inalienable right is to have a fate different from other people's. The skin on Hans' forehead and hands had been scraped and looked blue and red, the handsome features slumbered, the white lids covered the eyes and the half-open lips looked contented, almost cheerful. It seemed as if the boy's life had been nipped in the bud, as if a spectacular destiny had been thwarted, and his father in his fatigue and solitary grief succumbed to this happy delusion.

The funeral attracted a great number of curious onlookers. Hans Giebenrath had become a celebrity once again. The principal, the teachers and the pastor once more were involved in his fate. All of them were dressed in their best suits and solemn top hats. They accompanied the funeral procession and stopped for a moment at the graveside to whisper among themselves. The Latin teacher looked especially sad and the pastor said to him softly:

"Yes, Professor, he could have really become someone. Isn't it a shame that one has so much bad luck with the best of them?"

Along with the father and old Anna, who wept

without stopping, Master Flaig remained standing at the grave.

"Yes, something like that is rough, Herr Giebenrath," he said. "I was fond of the boy too."

"There's no understanding it," sighed Herr Giebenrath. "He was so talented and everything was going so well, the school, the examination—and then suddenly one misfortune after the other."

The shoemaker pointed after the frock coats disappearing through the churchyard gate.

"There you see a couple of gentlemen," he said softly, "who helped to put him where he is now."

"What?" Giebenrath exclaimed and gave the shoemaker a dubious, frightened look. "But, my God, how?"

"Take it easy, neighbor. I just meant the schoolmasters."

"But how? What do you mean?"

"Oh nothing. Perhaps you and I failed the boy in a number of ways too, don't you think?"

A serene blue sky stretched over the little town. The river glistened in the valley, the spruce-covered mountains yearned blue and soft into the distance. The shoemaker smiled sadly and took Herr Giebenrath's arm, the arm of a man who now walked with embarrassed, tentative steps out of this calm hour full of oddly painful thoughts down into the lowlands of his accustomed existence.

ABOUT THE AUTHOR

Born in 1877 in Calw, on the edge of the Black Forest, HERMANN HESSE was brought up in a missionary household where it was assumed that he would study for the ministry. Hesse's religious crisis (which is often recorded in his novels) led to his fleeing from the Maulbronn seminary in 1892, an unsuccessful cure by a well-known theologian and faith healer, and an attempted suicide. After being expelled from high school, he worked in bookshops for several years—a usual occupation for budding German authors.

His first novel, *Peter Camenzind* (1904), describes the early manhood of a writer who leaves his Swiss mountain village to encounter the world. This was followed by *Beneath the Wheel* (1906), the story of a gifted adolescent crushed by the brutal expectations of his father and teachers, a novel which was Hesse's personal attack on the educational system of his time.

World War I came as a terrific shock, and Hesse joined the pacifist Romain Rolland in antiwar activities—not only writing antiwar tracts and novels, but editing newspapers for German prisoners of war. During this period, Hesse's first marriage broke up (reflected or discussed outright in *Knulp* and *Rosshalde*), he studied the works of Freud, eventually underwent analysis with Jung, and was for a time a patient in a sanatorium.

In 1919 he moved permanently to Switzerland, and brought out *Demian*, which reflects his preoccupation with the workings of the subconscious and with psychoanalysis. The book was an enormous success, and made Hesse famous throughout Europe.

In 1922 he turned his attention to the East, which he had visited several times before the war, and wrote *Siddhartha*, the story of an Indian youth's long spiritual quest for the answer to the enigma of man's role on this earth. In 1927 he wrote *Steppenwolf*, the account of a man torn between his individualism and his attraction to bourgeois respectability, and his conflict between self-affirmation and self-destruction. In 1930 he published *Narcissus and Goldmund*, regarded as "Hesse's greatest novel" (*The New York Times*), dealing with the friendship between two medieval priests, one contented with his religion, the other a wanderer endlessly in search of peace and salvation.

The Journey to the East appeared in 1932, and there was no major work until 1943, when he brought out *Magister Ludi*, which won him the Nobel Prize in 1946. Until his death in 1962 he lived in seclusion in Montagnola, Switzerland.